T0115667

THE WIT AND WISDOM OF

BRIDGERTON

LADY WHISTLEDOWN'S

OFFICIAL GUIDE

AVON

An Imprint of HarperCollins*Publishers*

THE WIT AND WISDOM OF BRIDGERTON

JULIA QUINN

CONTENTS

INTRODUCTION

Dear Reader,

I come from a large family. Three sisters, a brother, various sisters- and brothers-in-law, nieces, nephews . . . and a positive flotilla of cousins. (I consider it a point of pride that one of my favorite people in the whole world is my *third* cousin.) Family events can be overwhelming —no one ever believes me when I say I'm the quiet one in the family— but they are always fun. We are silly, we are sharp, and we interrupt each other far more often than is polite.

We are never boring.

And we love each other. Fiercely.

I believe that this depth of unconditional support is something we all crave. And while we can rely on the promised Happily Ever After for each main couple in the Bridgerton books, I think that readers also long for the web of support that strongly wraps around a family like the Bridgertons. I'd like to think that if the Bridgertons were a contemporary family, they'd have such an active group text that everyone (especially Francesca) would have to turn off alerts. Violet, of course, would reign supreme with eight color-coordinated Google calendars.

I hope there is something in each of the characters that readers can identify with. Underneath the lighthearted narration lie real problems, real struggles and battles that, although set in the glamorous world of regency England, are still relevant and familiar to today's readers. Anthony grapples with the weight of sudden familial responsibility. Violet and Francesca must learn how to keep living after loss. Other characters struggle with issues of identity: Who are we outside of our assigned spot in our family? What does it mean to hide a piece of oneself from those who are closest to you? We can all recall moments when all we really wanted was simply to make sense of the world around us, to figure out who we were and who we wanted to be.

The Bridgertons, for all their privilege, are no different. And that's why we love them.

I am often asked if the actors on *Bridgerton* look the way they did in my head while writing them in the books. The answer is no, but only because I'm not a very visual writer, and I rarely have a clear sense of what my characters look like while I'm writing. (I rarely have even a fuzzy sense, to be honest; there's a reason I work with words and not pictures.) But as I went back through the books—from *The Duke and I* all the way to *On the Way to the Wedding*—to collect quotations for this volume, something interesting happened: I finally "saw" my characters. It didn't matter that I'd described Simon with blue eyes. In my head he was Regé-Jean Page. When Daphne smiled, I saw Phoebe Dynevor's face. I heard Adjoa Andoh in Lady Danbury's words, and it was Claudia Jessie's hand that scribbled the letters Eloise sent to her family. The television series has added a layer of richness to the books, just as I hope the books enhance the viewing experience. They are complements, in the very best sense of the word.

But this collection is focused on the books, and it is for that reason that you won't find some of your favorite Netflix moments in these pages. I've tried to assemble my favorite quotes from the Bridgerton novels, or at least the ones that best represent and illuminate each character. It wasn't easy; there were many passages that simply didn't work out of context. There were others that required light editing for clarity. In some places I've replaced a pronoun with a proper name. In others I've deleted an unnecessary sentence. Everyone got a brand-new *Whistledown* entry, which was tremendous fun for me—it's been well over a decade since I've picked up her quill.

A Bridgerton. To be such is to know that you are part of a family tightly webbed with staunch loyalty and unquestioning love. And laughter.

Always laughter.

Warmly,
Julia Quinn

THE WIT AND WISDOM OF

BRIDGERTON

1

ANTHONY

It is a dull week in London, so we shall recount one of the finer, more dashing moments of yesteryear about a gentleman now so staid and, dare we say it, *boringly* married that This Author has had no cause of late to include him in these papers.

Indeed, the Viscount Bridgerton has all but ceased to be newsworthy (a circumstance he likely appreciates). He dances with his wife so often that it is no longer scandalous. He dances with his mother, he dances with his sisters and his sister-in-law, and we presume he will someday dance with his daughter.

Positively tedious for a former rake who once was such a delight to write about.

But if This Author had to recount one moment that younger members of the *ton* might not have heard tell, and about which older members may have forgotten, it is the time he did *That Thing*. On *That Evening*.

It occurred at Aubrey Hall, the country seat of the Bridgerton family, and it would surely have been the talk of the season—or at least of a fortnight—except the following day the viscount found himself surprisingly engaged to be married amid undisclosed circumstances to a lady he'd not been courting.

Naturally, This Author chose to write about this shocking turn of events. And as a result, *That Thing* he did on *That Evening* went unreported.

But *That Thing* did happen, Dear Reader. And *That Evening* was glorious.

'Twas a house party thrown by his mother, the esteemed Lady Bridgerton, in which a positive gaggle of unmarried ladies were invited, and at which Lord Bridgerton, as host, was to escort some duchess or another into dinner.

But then Lord Bridgerton overheard one of the young misses make a vicious remark to another. Who the Injured Miss was is unimportant to the story, and who the Mean One was we shall not dignify. This story is about Anthony Bridgerton, and how he became a hero to wallflowers everywhere.

Standing more than a full head taller than the two ladies in question, Lord Bridgerton practically cast a shadow over the Mean One, gave her (Oh. My. Goodness!) the cut direct (Yes. He. Did!), and then indicated that he intended to escort the Injured Miss to dinner.

No, Dear Readers, This Author does not embellish.

Mean One then apparently blurted something akin to: "But you can't!"

Lord Bridgerton then said something to the effect of, "Was I talking to you?" and gave his undivided attention to the Injured Miss as he walked her into dinner, in front of everyone, with all the grace and deference as if she were a Princess of the Blood.

It was, Dear Reader, spectacular.

THE TOPIC of rakes has, of course, been previously discussed in this column, and This Author has come to the conclusion that there are rakes, and there are Rakes.

Anthony Bridgerton is a Rake.

A rake (lower-case) is youthful and immature. He flaunts his exploits, behaves with utmost idiocy, and thinks himself dangerous to women.

A Rake (upper-case) *knows* he is dangerous to women.

He doesn't flaunt his exploits because he doesn't need to. He knows he will be whispered about by men and women alike, and in fact, he'd rather they didn't whisper about him at all. He knows who he is and what he has done; further recountings are, to him, redundant.

He doesn't behave like an idiot for the simple reason that he isn't an idiot. He has little patience for the foibles of society, and quite frankly, most of the time This Author cannot say she blames him.

And if that doesn't describe Viscount Bridgerton—surely this season's most eligible bachelor—to perfection, This Author shall retire Her quill immediately.

LADY WHISTLEDOWN'S SOCIETY PAPERS

20 APRIL 1814

He was the firstborn Bridgerton of a firstborn Bridgerton of a firstborn Bridgerton eight times over. He had a dynastic responsibility to be fruitful and multiply.

Something had happened to him the night his father had died, when he'd remained in his parents' bedroom with the body, just sitting there for hours, watching his father and trying desperately to remember every moment they'd shared. It would be so easy to forget the little things—how Edmund would squeeze Anthony's upper arm when he needed encouragement. Or how he could recite from memory Balthazar's entire "Sigh No More," song from *Much Ado About Nothing*, not because he thought it particularly meaningful but just because he liked it.

And when Anthony finally emerged from the room, the first streaks of dawn pinking the sky, he somehow knew that his days were numbered, and numbered in the same way Edmund's had been.

He knew well the singularly strange sensation of loving one's family to distraction, and yet not feeling quite able to share one's deepest and most intractable fears. It brought on an uncanny sense of isolation, of being remarkably alone in a loud and loving crowd.

He was no fool; he knew that love existed. But he also believed in the power of the mind, and perhaps even more importantly, the power of the will. Frankly, he saw no reason why love should be an involuntary thing.

If he didn't want to fall in love, then by damn, he wasn't going to. It was as simple as that. It *had* to be as simple as that. If it weren't, then he wasn't much of a man, was he?

But the truth was, there was no one to blame, not even himself. It would make him feel so much better if he could point his finger at someone—anyone—and say, "This is *your* fault." It was juvenile, he knew, this need to assign blame, but everyone had a right to childish emotions from time to time, didn't they?

"Sometimes there are reasons for our fears that we can't quite explain. Sometimes it's just something we feel in our bones, something we know to be true, but would sound foolish to anyone else."

A MAN with charm is an entertaining thing, and a man with looks is, of course, a sight to behold, but a man with honor—ah, he is the one, Dear Reader, to which the young ladies should flock.

LADY WHISTLEDOWN'S SOCIETY PAPERS
2 MAY 1814

It was funny, he reflected later, how one's life could alter in an instant, how one minute everything could be a certain way, and the next it's simply . . . not.

The Viscount Who Loved Me

It was ironic, but death was the one thing he wasn't afraid of. Death wasn't frightening to a man alone. The great beyond held no terror when one had managed to avoid attachments here on earth.

Anthony could see Miss Sheffield growing worried at the devilish gleam in Colin's eye. He took a rather uncharitable pleasure in this. His reaction was, he knew, a touch out of proportion. But something about this Miss Katharine Sheffield sparked his temper and made him positively *itch* to do battle with her.

And win. That much went without saying.

"Oh, bloody hell," Anthony swore, completely forgetting that he was in the company of the woman he planned to make his wife. "She's got the mallet of death."

She wanted him. He knew enough of women to be positive of that. And by the time this night was through, she wouldn't be able to live without him.

That *he* might not be able to live without *her* was something he refused to consider.

“If I might offer you a piece of advice?” Colin said, munching on his walnut.

“You might not,” Anthony replied. He looked up. Colin was chewing with his mouth open. As this had been strictly forbidden while growing up in their household, Anthony could only deduce that Colin was displaying such poor manners only to make more noise. “Close your damned mouth,” he muttered.

Colin swallowed, smacked his lips, and took a sip of his tea to wash it all down. “Whatever you did, apologize for it. I know you, and I’m getting to know Kate, and knowing what I know—”

“What the hell is he talking about?” Anthony grumbled.

“I think,” Benedict said, leaning back in his chair, “that he’s telling you you’re an ass.”

THE DUKE AND I

“I was prepared to kill you for dishonoring her,” Anthony said to Simon. “If you damage her soul, I guarantee you will never find peace as long as you live. Which,” he added, his eyes turning slightly harder, “would not be long.”

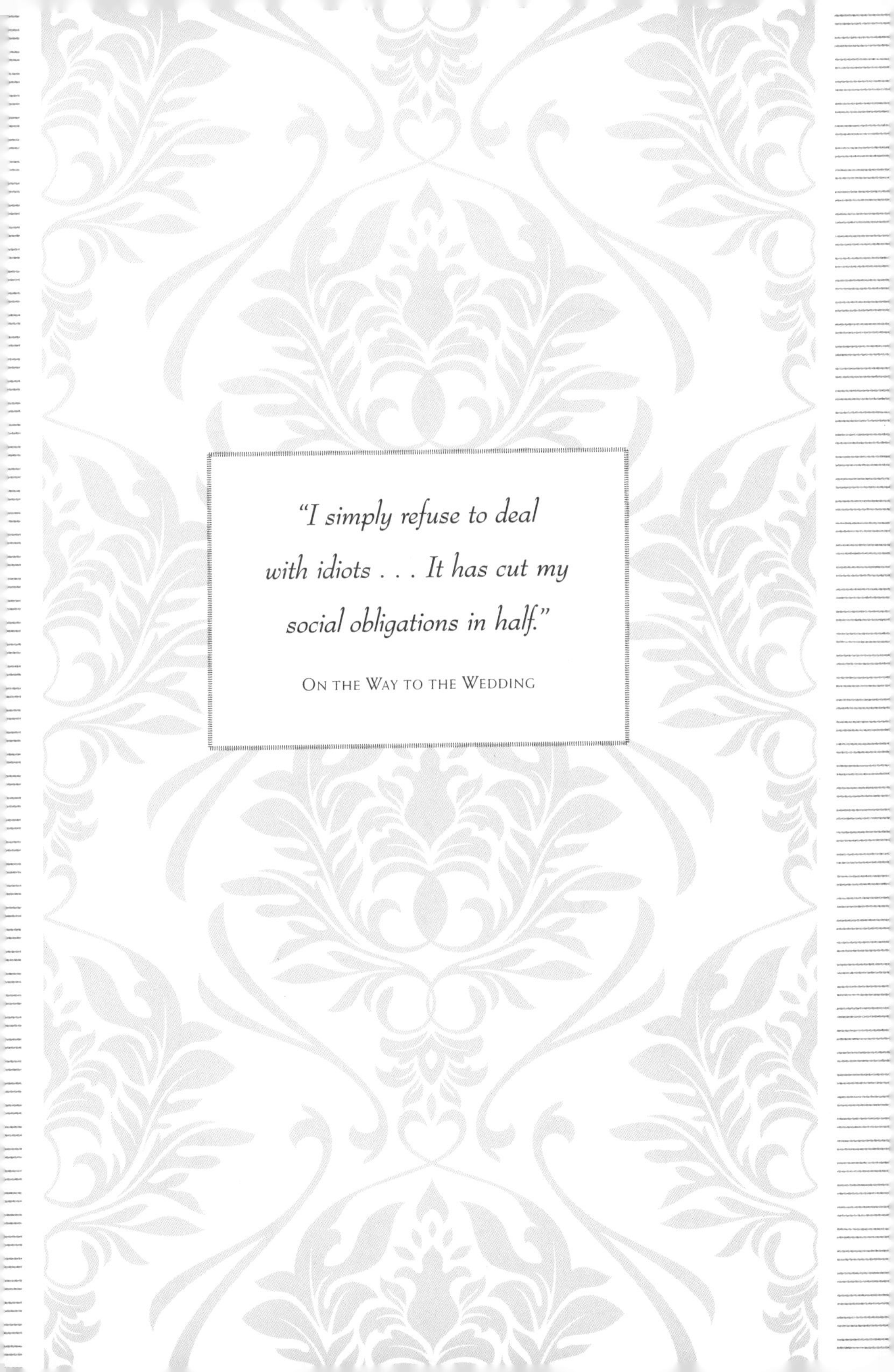

"I simply refuse to deal with idiots . . . It has cut my social obligations in half."

On the Way to the Wedding

THE VISCOUNT WHO LOVED ME

"You're far more caring a person than you'd like people to believe," Kate said.

Since he wasn't going to be able to win the argument with her—and there was little point in contradicting a woman when she was being complimentary—Anthony put a finger to his lips and said, "Shhh. Don't tell anyone."

"Listen to me," he said, his voice even and intense, "and listen well, because I'm only going to say this once. I desire you. I burn for you. I can't sleep at night for wanting you. Even when I didn't *like* you, I lusted for you. It's the most maddening, beguiling, damnable thing, but there it is. And if I hear one more word of nonsense from your lips, I'm going to have to tie you to the bloody bed and have my way with you a hundred different ways, until you finally get it through your silly skull that you are the most beautiful and desirable woman in England, and if everyone else doesn't see that, then they're all bloody fools."

"Love isn't about being afraid that it will all be snatched away. Love's about finding the one person who makes your heart complete, who makes you a better person than you ever dreamed you could be. It's about looking in the eyes of your wife and knowing, all the way to your bones, that she's simply the best person you've ever known."

IT'S IN HIS KISS

"My sister Hyacinth," the viscount said slowly, walking toward the window, "is a prize. You should remember that, and if you value your skin, you will treat her as the treasure she is."

Gareth held his tongue. It didn't seem the correct time to chime in.

"But while Hyacinth may be a prize," Anthony said, turning around with the slow, deliberate steps of a man who is well familiar with his power, "she isn't easy. I will be the first one to admit to this. There aren't many men who can match wits with her, and if she is trapped into marriage with someone who does not appreciate her . . . singular personality, she will be miserable."

Still, Gareth did not speak. But he did not remove his eyes from the viscount's face.

And Anthony returned the gesture. "I will give you my permission to marry her," he said. "But you should think long and hard before you ask her yourself."

"What are you saying?" Gareth asked suspiciously, rising to his feet.

"I will not mention this interview to her. It is up to you to decide if you wish to take the final step. And if you do not . . ." The viscount shrugged, his shoulders rising and falling in an oddly Gallic gesture. "In that case," he said, sounding almost disturbingly calm, "she will never know."

How many men had the viscount scared off in this manner, Gareth wondered. Good God, was this why Hyacinth had gone unmarried for so long? He supposed he should be grateful, since it had left her free to marry him, but still, did she realize her eldest brother was a *madman*?

"If you don't make my sister happy," Anthony Bridgerton continued, his eyes just intense enough to confirm Gareth's suspicions about his sanity, "then *you* will not be happy. I will see to it myself."

TO SIR PHILLIP, WITH LOVE

"You are a Bridgerton. I don't care who you marry or what your name becomes when you stand up before a priest and say your vows. You will always be a Bridgerton, and we behave with honor and honesty, not because it is expected of us, but because *that is what we are*."

ANTHONY, ACCORDING TO HIS FAMILY . . .

"I'm thankful every day I wasn't born in
Anthony's shoes. . . . The title, the family, the fortune—
it's a great deal to fit on one man's shoulders."

COLIN, *The Viscount Who Loved Me*

Anthony's arms were crossed, never a good sign.
Anthony was the Viscount Bridgerton, and had been for
more than twenty years. And while he was, Gregory would
be the first to insist, the very best of brothers, he would
have made a rather fine feudal lord.

On the Way to the Wedding

"If Anthony isn't a rake, I pity the
woman who meets the man who is."

SIMON, *The Duke and I*

"No one smirks quite like my eldest brother."

DAPHNE, *The Viscount Who Loved Me*

2

KATE

Weddings are a frequent topic within these pages, but wedding presents are not—until now. It seems that Lady Bridgerton (current, not dowager) has bestowed upon her niece a most curious nuptial gift. The niece in question is Lady Alexandra Rokesby, who enjoyed a quiet but successful season last year under the expert eye of the other Lady Bridgerton (dowager, not current). Lady Alexandra, it seems, has also spent many an idyllic afternoon with her Bridgerton cousins at Aubrey Hall, in Kent.

It is worth noting that when Bridgertons gather in the countryside, they like to play Pall Mall.

There are nuances to this tale that only a Bridgerton might understand, but Pall Mall is apparently something they take very seriously. This Author has it on the best authority that there is no player more fiercely competitive than Lady Bridgerton (current, not dowager) herself.

This is where the tale grows strange. During one of these games, Kate (as Lady Bridgerton is known to her family) presented to Alexandra a black mallet. The significance of this gesture is beyond This Author's ability to discern, but significant it must have been, as the moment was met with gasps of astonishment amongst the (Bridgertonian) crowd. And surely it cannot be a coincidence that Lord Bridgerton was seen later that afternoon knee-deep in the lake.

And the wedding gift? Not the original mallet; that, we are told, was merely a ceremonial gesture. Instead, Lady Bridgerton commissioned an elegant Pall Mall set from a master in Milan. Containing a black mallet with lettering engraved in gold. *Gold*, Dear Reader!

What might be so extravagantly engraved upon the mallet? Only Lady Bridgerton knows . . .

THE VISCOUNT WHO LOVED ME

Kate stood with her shoulders straight and tall, couldn't sit still if her life depended upon it, and walked as if she were in a race—and why not, she always wondered, if one was going somewhere, what could possibly be the point in not getting there quickly?

"I am Edwina's older sister. I have always had to be strong for her. Whereas she has only had to be strong for herself."

Kate caught the smile in his eyes and realized Colin had been bamming her all along. This was not a man who wished his brothers off to perdition. "You're rather devoted to your family, aren't you?" she asked.

His eyes, which had been laughing throughout the conversation, turned dead serious without even a blink. "Utterly."

"As am I," Kate said pointedly.

"And that means?"

"It means," she said, knowing she should hold her tongue but speaking anyway, "that I will not allow anyone to break my sister's heart."

VISCOUNT BRIDGERTON was also seen dancing with Miss Katharine Sheffield, elder sister to the fair Edwina. This can only mean one thing, as it has not escaped the notice of This Author that the elder Miss Sheffield has been in much demand on the dance floor ever since the younger Miss Sheffield made her bizarre and unprecedented announcement at the Smythe-Smith musicale last week.

Whoever heard of a girl needing her sister's permission to choose a husband?

LADY WHISTLEDOWN'S SOCIETY PAPERS
22 APRIL 1814

THE DEED is done! Miss Sheffield is now Katharine, Viscountess Bridgerton.

This Author extends the very best of wishes to the happy couple. Sensible and honorable people are surely scarce among the *ton*, and it's certainly gratifying to see two of this rare breed joined in marriage.

LADY WHISTLEDOWN'S SOCIETY PAPERS
16 MAY 1814

It was inconceivable to Anthony that Kate Sheffield, for all her wit and intelligence, could *not* be jealous of her sister. And even if there was nothing she could have done to prevent this mishap, surely she must be taking a bit of pleasure in the fact that she was dry and comfortable while Edwina looked like a drowned rat. An attractive rat, to be sure, but certainly a drowned one.

But Kate clearly wasn't done with the conversation. "Aside from the fact," she scorned, "that I would never ever do anything to harm Edwina, how do you propose I managed this amazing feat?" She clapped her free hand to her cheek in an expression of mock discovery. "Oh, yes, I know the secret language of the corgis. I ordered the dog to yank the lead from my hand and then, since I have the second sight, I knew that Edwina was standing right here by The Serpentine so then I said to the dog—through our powerful mind-to-mind connection, since he was much too far away to hear my voice at this point—to change his direction, head for Edwina, and topple her into the lake."

"Sarcasm doesn't become you, Miss Sheffield."

"*Nothing* becomes you, Lord Bridgerton."

No one had ever brought her flowers before, and she hadn't known until that very moment how badly she'd wanted someone to do so.

Suddenly it was too hard to be in his presence, too painful to know that he would belong to someone else.

"Why," Edwina whispered in Kate's ear, "do I get the feeling I am intruding upon a family spat?"

"I think the Bridgertons take Pall Mall very seriously," Kate whispered back. The three Bridgerton siblings had assumed bulldog faces, and they all appeared rather single-mindedly determined to win.

"Eh eh eh!" Colin scolded, waving a finger at them. "No collusion allowed."

"We wouldn't even begin to know where to collude," Kate commented, "as no one has seen fit to even explain to us the rules of play."

"Just follow along," Daphne said briskly. "You'll figure it out as you go."

"I think," Kate whispered to Edwina, "that the object is to sink your opponents' balls into the lake."

"Really?"

"No. But I think that's how the Bridgertons see it."

IT HAS come to This Author's attention that Miss Katharine Sheffield took offense at the labeling of her beloved pet, "an unnamed dog of indeterminate breed."

This Author is, to be sure, prostrate with shame at this grievous and egregious error and begs of you, Dear Reader, to accept this abject apology and pay attention to the first ever correction in the history of this column.

Miss Katharine Sheffield's dog is a corgi. It is called Newton, although it is difficult to imagine that England's great inventor and physicist would have appreciated being immortalized in the form of a short, fat canine with poor manners.

LADY WHISTLEDOWN'S SOCIETY PAPERS
17 APRIL 1814

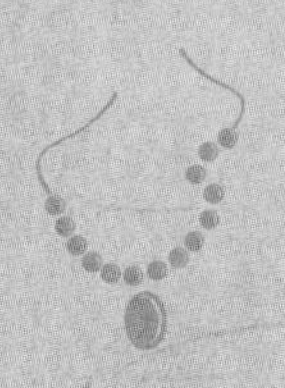

Kate didn't believe for one second that reformed rakes made the best husbands. She wasn't even sure that a rake could be properly reformed in the first place.

The Viscount Who Loved Me

❁

Anthony looked down to where the wooden balls sat kissing on the grass, hers black, his appallingly pink. . . . He put his foot atop his ball, drew back his mallet—

"What are you doing?" Kate shrieked.

—and let fly. His ball remained firmly in place under his boot. Hers went sailing down the hill for what seemed like miles.

"You fiend," she growled.

"All's fair in love and war," he quipped.

"I am going to *kill* you."

"You can try," he taunted, "but you'll have to catch up with me first."

Kate pondered the mallet of death, then pondered his foot.

"Don't even think about it," he warned.

"It's so very, very tempting," she growled.

He leaned forward menacingly. "We have witnesses."

"And that is the only thing saving your life right now."

"You don't want to do this, Miss Sheffield," Anthony warned.

"Oh," she said with great feeling, "I *do*. I really, really do." And then, with quite the most evil grin her lips had ever formed, she drew back her mallet and smacked her ball with every ounce of every single emotion within her. It knocked into his with stunning force, sending it hurtling even further down the hill.

Further . . .

Further . . .

Right into the lake.

Openmouthed with delight, Kate just stared for a moment as the pink ball sank into the lake. Then, something rose up within her, some strange and primitive emotion, and before she knew what she was about, she was jumping about like a crazy woman, yelling, "Yes! Yes! I win!"

"You don't win," Anthony snapped.

"Oh, it *feels* like I've won," she reveled.

"Do you miss a parent you never knew?" Anthony whispered.

Kate considered his question for some time. His voice had held a hoarse urgency that told her there was something critical about her reply. Why, she couldn't imagine, but something about her childhood clearly rang a chord within his heart.

"Yes," she finally answered, "but not in the way you would think. You can't really miss her, because you didn't know her, but there's still a hole in your life—a big empty spot, and you know who was supposed to fit there, but you can't remember her, and you don't know what she was like, and so you don't know *how* she would have filled that hole." Her lips curved into a sad sort of smile. "Does this make any sense?"

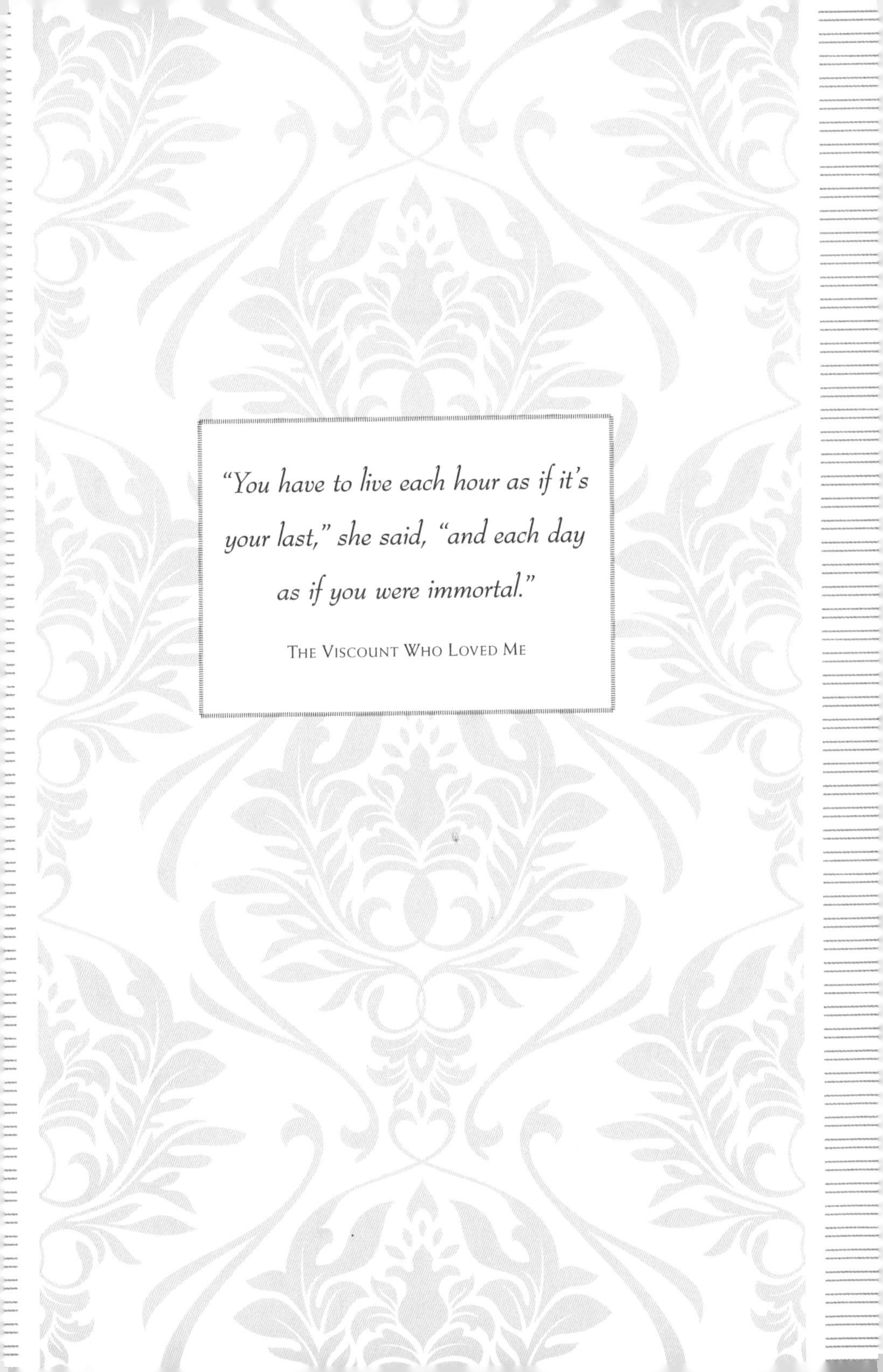
"You have to live each hour as if it's your last," she said, "and each day as if you were immortal."
THE VISCOUNT WHO LOVED ME

THERE IS nothing like a spot of competition to bring out the worst in a man—or the best in a woman.

LADY WHISTLEDOWN'S SOCIETY PAPERS
4 MAY 1814

When Anthony kissed her, she felt as if she were losing her mind. And when he kissed her twice, she wasn't even sure if she wanted it back!

Kate stared at him intently, watching his dark eyes in the flickering candlelight, and catching her breath at the flash of pain she saw in the brief second before he looked away. And she knew—with every fiber of her being—that he wasn't speaking of intangibles. He was talking about his own fears, something very specific that haunted him every minute of every day.

Something she knew she did not have the right to ask him about. But she wished—oh, how she wished—that when he was ready to face his fears, she could be the one to help him.

Was it possible to fall in love with the same man over and over again, every single day?

ON THE WAY TO THE WEDDING

Gregory turned to Kate. "You have no arguments with this?"

"Oh, I have many arguments," she answered, craning her neck as she examined the ballroom for any last minute disasters. "I always have arguments."

"It's true," Anthony said. "But she knows when she cannot win."

Kate turned to Gregory even though her words were quite clearly directed at her husband. "What I *know* is how to choose my battles."

"Pay her no mind," Anthony said. "That is just her way of admitting defeat."

"And yet he continues," Kate said to no one in particular, "even though he knows that I always win in the end."

KATE, ACCORDING TO HER FAMILY . . .

. . . you do have the right of it, dearest Kate.
Men are so easy to manage. I cannot imagine
ever losing an argument with one.

FROM ELOISE BRIDGERTON, TO HER SISTER-IN-LAW
VISCOUNTESS BRIDGERTON, UPON REFUSING HER
FIFTH OFFER OF MARRIAGE

To Sir Phillip, With Love

"When you agree to be mother to a child you haven't borne,
your responsibility is twice as great. You must work even
harder to ensure that child's happiness and welfare."

MARY, *The Viscount Who Loved Me*

"Were *you* tempted by the barmaid?" Eloise asked.
Anthony was aghast. "Of course not!
Kate would slit my throat."
"I'm not talking about what Kate would do to you
if you strayed, although I'm of the opinion that she
would not start at your throat—"

To Sir Phillip, With Love

"I knew you were worthy of the mallet of death."

COLIN, *The Viscount Who Loved Me*

3

BENEDICT

Mr. Benedict Bridgerton, second eldest of the Bridgerton brood, is quite the accomplished artist. This Author was aware that Mr. Bridgerton dabbled in sketching with charcoals, as he mentioned such in passing at the Hastings House Ball last year. He was characteristically understated in this disclosure; the second Bridgerton brother is not known to draw attention to himself.

But painting? Lo and beyond, this is not the drab watercolors as ladies of the *ton* are dutifully schooled in, but landscapes rich and lush in oils. And while This Author has not seen these paintings, a rumor has been circulating that his talent may be enough to earn some wall space in the National Gallery.

Mr. Bridgerton, married just over a year ago to the former Miss Sophia Beckett, a distant relation to the Earl of Penwood, is an infrequent guest in London during the season. He and his wife are said to prefer the country and reside in a small but well-appointed cottage just outside of Rosemeade. This Author imagines there is a well-lit artist's studio there, with French doors opening to all that is pastoral and bucolic. But as This Author has never been invited, she can only speculate.

That said, This Author's speculations are usually uncannily accurate.

AN OFFER FROM A GENTLEMAN

Benedict was a Bridgerton, and while there was no family to which he'd rather belong, he sometimes wished he were considered a little less a Bridgerton and a little more himself.

He'd turned and seen her, and he'd known she was the reason he was there that night; the reason he lived in England; hell, the very reason he'd been born.

She was out there somewhere. He'd long since resigned himself to the fact that he wasn't likely to find her, and he hadn't searched actively for over a year, but . . .

He just couldn't stop from looking. It had become, in a very strange way, a part of who he was. His name was Benedict Bridgerton, he had seven brothers and sisters, was rather skilled with both a sword and a sketching crayon, and he always kept his eyes open for the one woman who had touched his soul.

MORE THAN one masquerade attendee has reported to This Author that Benedict Bridgerton was seen in the company of an unknown lady dressed in a silver gown.

Try as she might, This Author has been completely unable to discern the mystery lady's identity. And if This Author cannot uncover the truth, you may be assured that her identity is a well-kept secret indeed.

LADY WHISTLEDOWN'S SOCIETY PAPERS
7 JUNE 1815

It seemed an unwritten rule that all ladies of the *ton* must keep their callers waiting for at least fifteen minutes, twenty if they were feeling particularly peevish.

A bloody stupid rule, Benedict thought. Why the rest of the world didn't value punctuality as he did, he would never know.

Now, as he stood in the pond, the water lapping at his midriff, just above his navel, he was struck once again by that odd sense of somehow being more alive than he'd been just seconds earlier. It was a good feeling, an exciting, breathless rush of emotion.

It was like before. When he'd met *her.*

Something was about to happen, or maybe someone was near.

His life was about to change.

And he was, he realized with a wry twist of his lips, naked as the day he was born.

"I think I *have* to kiss you," Benedict said, looking as if he couldn't quite believe his own words. "It's rather like breathing. One doesn't have much choice in the matter."

"Whatever could you be thinking," Benedict mused, "to look so adorably ferocious? No, don't tell me," he added. "I'm sure it involves my untimely and painful demise."

He knew—absolutely knew—that if one of them didn't leave the room in the next thirty seconds, he was going to do something for which he'd owe her a thousand apologies.

Not that he didn't plan to seduce her. Just that he'd rather do it with a bit more finesse.

"Sometimes," Benedict said, keeping his voice purposefully light and gentle, "it's not so easy being a Bridgerton."

Her head slowly turned around. "I can't imagine anything nicer."

"There isn't anything nicer," he replied, "but that doesn't mean it's always easy."

"What do you mean?"

And Benedict found himself giving voice to feelings he'd never shared with any other living soul, not even—no, especially not his family. "To most of the world," he said, "I'm merely a Bridgerton. I'm not Benedict or Ben or even a gentleman of means and hopefully a bit of intelligence. I'm merely"—he smiled ruefully—"a Bridgerton. Specifically, Number Two."

BENEDICT BRIDGERTON is apparently in London, but he eschews all polite social gatherings in favor of less genteel milieus.

Although if truth be told, This Author should not give the impression that the aforementioned Mr. Bridgerton has been spending his every waking hour in debauched abandon. If accounts are correct, he has spent most of the past fortnight in his lodgings on Bruton Street.

As there have been no rumors that he is ill, This Author can only assume that he has finally come to the conclusion that the London season is utterly dull and not worth his time.

Smart man, indeed.

LADY WHISTLEDOWN'S SOCIETY PAPERS
9 JUNE 1817

"If you like your life dull,
then that can only mean that
you do not understand the
nature of excitement."

An Offer From a Gentleman

Benedict stood immediately. Certain manners could be ignored for one's sister, but never for one's mother.

"I saw your feet on the table," Violet said before he could even open his mouth.

"I was merely polishing the surface with my boots."

"What are you up to?" Sophie asked.

"Why would you think I'm up to anything?"

Her lips pursed before she said, "You wouldn't be you if you weren't up to something."

Benedict smiled at that. "I do believe that was a compliment."

"It wasn't necessarily intended as such."

"But nonetheless," he said mildly, "that's how I choose to take it."

"I promise that your virtue will be safe," he interrupted. And then he added, because he couldn't quite help himself: "Unless *you* want it otherwise."

"So now you're jumping out at me from *closets*?"

"Of course not." He looked affronted. "That was a staircase."

He was, he realized, comforted by her presence. They didn't need to talk. They didn't even need to touch (although he wasn't about to let go just then). Simply put, he was a happier man—and quite possibly a better man—when she was near.

She was here, with him, and she felt like heaven. The soft scent of her hair, the slight taste of salt on her skin—she was, he thought, born to rest in the shelter of his arms. And he was born to hold her.

"When I thought about what it was in life I really needed—not what I wanted, but what I needed—the only thing that kept coming up was you."

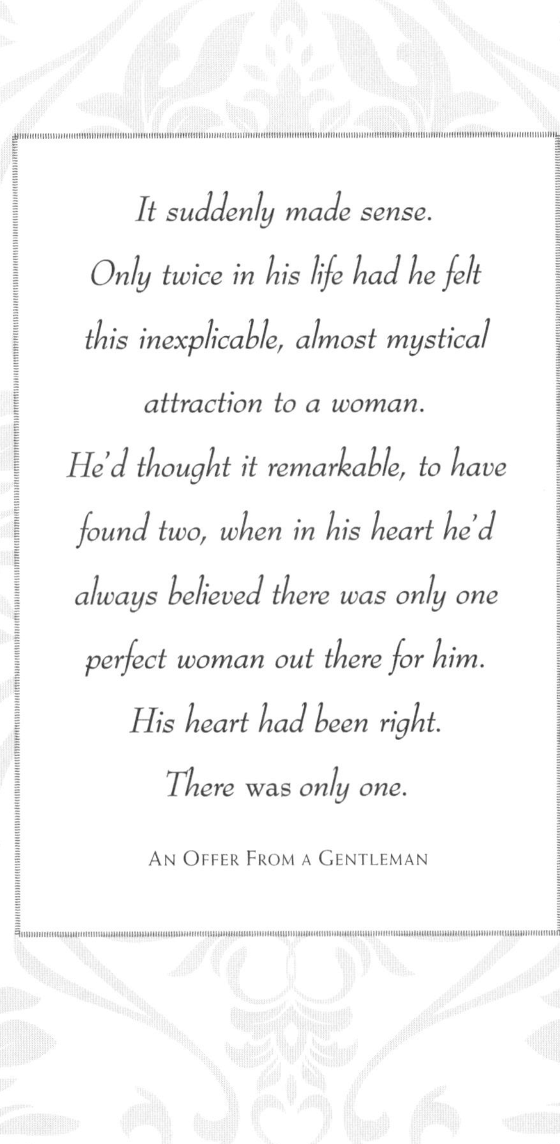

It suddenly made sense.
Only twice in his life had he felt
this inexplicable, almost mystical
attraction to a woman.
He'd thought it remarkable, to have
found two, when in his heart he'd
always believed there was only one
perfect woman out there for him.
His heart had been right.
There was only one.

AN OFFER FROM A GENTLEMAN

BENEDICT, ACCORDING TO HIS FAMILY . . .

"Benedict always loves to natter on about art.
I rarely am able to follow the conversation,
but he seems quite animated."

GREGORY, *On the Way to the Wedding*

"Love grows and changes every day. And it isn't like
some thunderbolt from the sky, instantly transforming
you into a different man. I know Benedict says it was
that way for him, and that's just lovely,
but you know, Benedict is *not* normal."

DAPHNE, *Romancing Mister Bridgerton*

4

COLIN

What is the mark of a gentleman? Many would say style, and surely Mr. Beau Brummell would agree, had he not fled the country in the wake of unpaid debts two years ago. Others might point to intellect, a flair of the word, so to speak. Lord Byron would do nicely within the boundaries of this definition . . . had he not also fled the country.

Also for unpaid debts.

Also two years ago.

'Tis a positive epidemic of gentlemen departing our shores, although This Author must take pains to point out that while Colin Bridgerton plans to depart for Denmark later this month, he is neither a borrower nor a lender. His is a trip of pleasure, as are all his travels.

The ladies of the *ton* shall surely mourn his absence, but to his own self Mr. Bridgerton must be true. His love of travel is well-established. Almost as well-established as his cheeky grin and flirtatious manner. This Author is far too busy to count the number of broken hearts Mr. Bridgerton has left strewn across London, but it must be said that none of these shattered organs were the result of malicious or salacious actions by Mr. Bridgerton.

Alas, he needs not to *do* to make the ladies fall in love. He merely needs to *be*.

If brevity is indeed the soul of wit, This Author shall say only—perhaps this is why he so often flees our shores.

ROMANCING MISTER BRIDGERTON

Colin Bridgerton was famous for many things.

He was famous for his good looks, which was no surprise; all the Bridgerton men were famous for their good looks.

He was famous for his slightly crooked smile, which could melt a woman's heart across a crowded ballroom and had even once caused a young lady to faint dead away, or at least to swoon delicately, then hit her head on a table, which did produce the aforementioned dead faint.

He was famous for his mellow charm, his ability to set anyone at ease with a smooth grin and an amusing comment.

What he was *not* famous for, and in fact what many people would have sworn he did not even possess, was a temper.

THE DUKE AND I

"I hope he knows what he has in you," Colin said quietly to Daphne. "Because if he doesn't, I may have to shoot him myself."

MATCHMAKING MAMAS are united in their glee—Colin Bridgerton has returned from Greece!

For those gentle (and ignorant) readers who are new to town this year, Mr. Bridgerton is third in the legendary string of eight Bridgerton siblings (hence the name Colin, beginning with C; he follows Anthony and Benedict, and precedes Daphne, Eloise, Francesca, Gregory, and Hyacinth.)

Although Mr. Bridgerton holds no noble title and is unlikely ever to do so (he is seventh in line for the title of Viscount Bridgerton, behind the two sons of the current viscount, his elder brother Benedict, and his three sons) he is still considered one of the prime catches of the season, due to his fortune, his face, his form, and most of all, his charm.

LADY WHISTLEDOWN'S SOCIETY PAPERS
2 APRIL 1824

ROMANCING MISTER BRIDGERTON

"You're a terrible liar, did you know that?"

He straightened, tugging slightly at his waistcoat as he lifted his chin. "Actually, I'm an excellent liar. But what I'm really good at is appearing appropriately sheepish and adorable after I'm caught."

What, Penelope wondered, was she meant to say to *that*? Because surely there was no one more adorably sheepish (sheepishly adorable?) than Colin Bridgerton with his hands clasped behind his back, his eyes flitting along the ceiling, and his lips puckered into an innocent whistle.

Colin knew the *ton* well. He knew how his peers acted. The aristocracy was capable of individual greatness, but collectively they tended to sink to the lowest common denominator.

FIRST COMES SCANDAL

"Hold the baby, would you?" Violet thrust Colin forward, and Georgie had no choice but to take him.

He immediately began to scream.

"I think he's hungry," Georgie said.

"He's *always* hungry. Honestly, I don't know what to do with him. He ate half of my meat pasty yesterday."

Georgie sent a horrified look at her little nephew. "Does he even have teeth?"

"No," Violet replied. "He just gummed the whole thing down."

ROMANCING MISTER BRIDGERTON

It was quite strange, actually, how he loved returning home just as much as he did the departure.

Colin had never been opposed to marriage. He'd simply been opposed to a dull marriage.

"And here I thought I was inscrutable."

"Afraid not," she replied. "Not to me, anyway."

Colin sighed. "I fear it will never be my destiny to be a dark, brooding hero."

"You may well find yourself *some*one's hero," Penelope allowed. "There's time for you yet. But dark and brooding?" She smiled. "Not very likely."

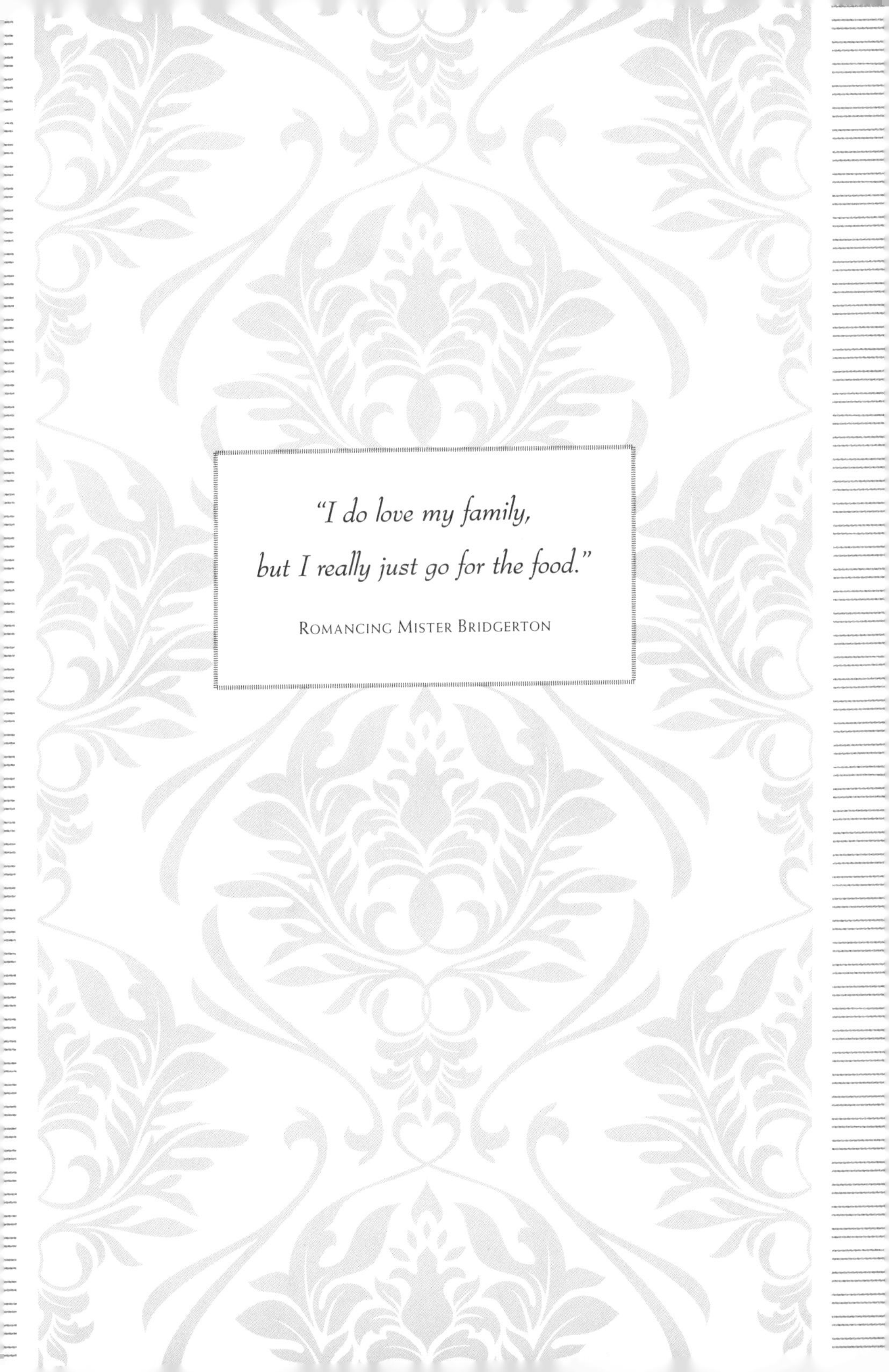

"I do love my family,
but I really just go for the food."

Romancing Mister Bridgerton

Colin decided then and there that the female mind was a strange and incomprehensible organ—one which no man should even attempt to understand. There wasn't a woman alive who could go from point A to B without stopping at C, D, X, and 12 along the way.

Romancing Mister Bridgerton

"A man can't travel forever; to do so would take all the fun out of it."

Suddenly he didn't know what to say. Which was strange, because he *always* knew what to say. In fact, he was somewhat famous for always knowing what to say. It was, he reflected, probably one of the reasons he was so well liked.

But he sensed that Penelope's feelings depended on his next words, and at some point in the last ten minutes, her feelings had become very important to him.

THE VISCOUNT WHO LOVED ME

"Honor and honesty has its time and place, but *not* in a game of Pall Mall."

ROMANCING MISTER BRIDGERTON

"Mother," he said, turning toward Violet, "how have you been?"

"You've been sending cryptic notes all over town," Violet demanded, "and you want to know how I've *been*?"

He smiled. "Yes."

Violet actually started wagging her finger at him, something she'd forbidden her own children from ever doing in public. "Oh, no you don't, Colin Bridgerton. You are not going to get out of explaining yourself. I am your mother. Your mother!"

"I am aware of the relation," he murmured.

"Biscuits are good," Hyacinth said, thrusting a plate in Penelope's direction.

"Hyacinth," Lady Bridgerton said in a vaguely disapproving voice, "do try to speak in complete sentences."

Hyacinth looked at her mother with a surprised expression. "Biscuits. Are. Good." She cocked her head to the side. "Noun. Verb. Adjective."

"*Hyacinth.*"

"Noun. Verb. Adjective," Colin said, wiping a crumb from his grinning face. "Sentence. Is. Correct."

ON THE WAY TO THE WEDDING

Gregory had told Colin everything, even down to the events of the night before. He did not like telling tales of Lucy, but one really could not ask one's brother to sit in a tree for hours without explaining why. And Gregory had found a certain comfort in unburdening himself to Colin. He had not lectured. He had not judged.

In fact, he had understood.

When Gregory had finished his tale, tersely explaining why he was waiting outside Fennsworth House, Colin had simply nodded and said, "I don't suppose you have something to eat."

Gregory shook his head and grinned.

It was good to have a brother.

"Rather poor planning on your part," Colin muttered.

ROMANCING MISTER BRIDGERTON

Everything he thought he'd known about kissing was rubbish.

Everything else had been mere lips and tongue and softly murmured but meaningless words.

This was a kiss.

There was something in the friction, the way he could hear and feel her breath at the same time. Something in the way she held perfectly still, and yet he could feel her heart pounding through her skin.

There was something in the fact that he knew it was *her*.

He assumed he'd say something flip and droll, like the devil-may-care fellow he was reputed to be. "This means nothing," perhaps, echoing her own sentiments, or maybe, "Every woman deserves at least one kiss." But as he closed the bare distance between them, he realized that there were no words that could capture the intensity of the moment.

No words for the passion. No words for the need.

No words for the sheer epiphany of the moment.

And so, on an otherwise unremarkable Friday afternoon, in the heart of Mayfair, in a quiet drawing room on Mount Street, Colin Bridgerton kissed Penelope Featherington.

And it was glorious.

And that was when he realized that Daphne had been right. His love hadn't been a thunderbolt from the sky. It had started with a smile, a word, a teasing glance. Every second he had spent in her presence it had grown, until he'd reached this moment, and he suddenly *knew*.

TO SIR PHILLIP, WITH LOVE

"How can you think of food?" Gregory said angrily.

"I always think of food," Colin replied, his eyes searching the table until he located the butter. "What else is there?"

"Your wife," Benedict drawled.

"Ah, yes, my wife," Colin said with a nod. He turned to Phillip, leveled a hard stare at him, and said, "Just so that you are aware, I would have rather spent the night with my wife."

Phillip couldn't think of a reply that might not hint at insult to the absent Mrs. Bridgerton, so he just nodded and buttered a roll of his own.

Colin took a huge bite, then spoke with his mouth full, the etiquette breach a clear insult to his host. "We've only been married a few weeks."

Phillip raised one of his brows in question.

"Still newlyweds."

Phillip nodded, since some sort of response seemed to be required.

Colin leaned forward. "I *really* did not want to leave my wife."

"I see," Phillip murmured, since truly, what else could he have said?

"Do you understand what he's saying?" Gregory demanded.

Colin turned and sent a chilling look at his brother, who was clearly too young to have mastered the fine art of nuance and circumspect speech. Phillip waited until Colin had turned back to the table, offered him a plate of asparagus (which he took), then said, "I gather you miss your wife."

There was a beat of silence, and then Colin said, after sending one last disdainful glance at his brother, "Indeed."

ROMANCING MISTER BRIDGERTON

"I love you with everything I am, everything I've been, and everything I hope to be. I love you with my past, and I love you for my future. I love you for the children we'll have and for the years we'll have together. I love you for every one of my smiles and even more, for every one of your smiles."

COLIN, ACCORDING TO HIS FAMILY . . .

"*Colin* is your favorite brother?"

SIMON, *The Duke and I*

When Phillip smiled . . . Eloise suddenly understood what all those young ladies were talking about when they'd waxed rhapsodic over her brother Colin's smile (which Eloise found rather ordinary; it was *Colin*, after all).

To Sir Phillip, With Love

Even Colin—the golden boy, the man with the easy smile and devilish humor—had raw spots of his own. He was haunted by unfulfilled dreams and secret insecurities. How unfair she had been when she'd pondered his life, not to allow him his weaknesses.

PENELOPE, *Romancing Mister Bridgerton*

"Shall we return to the dining room?" Anthony queried. "I imagine you're hungry, and if we tarry much longer, Colin is sure to have eaten our host out of house and home."

To Sir Phillip, With Love

PENELOPE

Miss Penelope Featherington was spotted in Mayfair with Lady Louisa McCann and quite possibly the fattest dog This Author has ever seen. But the news to report of Miss Featherington is neither the company of the Duke of Fenniwick's daughter nor her utter chunk of a canine. (Lady Louisa's, that is; Miss Featherington does own a dog, but it is of quite normal girth.)

No, the grand news of the day was the astonishingly palatable color of her day dress—not a single yellow thread to be seen. While it is true that Miss Featherington's attire has consisted of cooler tones these past few years, it is impossible to excise from one's memory the lemons and oranges of the lady's inauspicious debut. Some may have judged it cruel to have compared Miss Featherington to an "overripe citrus fruit," but This Author maintains that the color of sunshine is deeply unflattering to many complexions. Indeed, even the esteemed Lady Bridgerton was (back when she was merely Miss Sheffield) likened to a "singed daffodil."

But alas, has this change of wardrobe come too late for Miss Featherington? Is the lady—now firmly on the darker side of twenty-five—on the shelf? Some would say yes. In fact, most would say yes. But if she were to find herself on the receiving end of a suitor's pursuit, she would not be the first spinster to surprise the *ton*. After all, Miss Eloise Bridgerton is almost precisely the same age as Miss Penelope Featherington, and she has received two marriage proposals in the past two years.

Perhaps Penelope will yet surprise us all . . .

Or perhaps not.

LADY WHISTLEDOWN'S SOCIETY PAPERS, 1822

Deep inside, she knew who she was, and that person was smart and kind and often even funny, but somehow her personality always got lost somewhere between her heart and her mouth, and she found herself saying the wrong thing or, more often, nothing at all.

On the sixth of April, in the year 1812—precisely two days before her sixteenth birthday—Penelope Featherington fell in love.

It was, in a word, thrilling. The world shook. Her heart leaped. The moment was breathtaking. And, she was able to tell herself with some satisfaction, the man in question—one Colin Bridgerton—felt precisely the same way.

Oh, not the love part. He certainly didn't fall in love with her in 1812 (and not in 1813, 1814, 1815, or—oh blast, not in all the years 1816–1822, either, and certainly not in 1823, when he was out of the country the whole time, anyway). But his earth shook, his heart leaped, and Penelope knew without a shadow of a doubt that his breath was taken away as well. For a good ten seconds.

Falling off a horse tended to do that to a man.

La, but such excitement yesterday on the front steps of Lady Bridgerton's residence on Bruton Street!

First, Penelope Featherington was seen in the company of not one, not two, but THREE Bridgerton brothers, surely a heretofore impossible feat for the poor girl, who is rather infamous for her wallflower ways. Sadly (but perhaps predictably) for Miss Featherington, when she finally departed, it was on the arm of the viscount, the only married man in the bunch.

If Miss Featherington were to somehow manage to drag a Bridgerton brother to the altar, it would surely mean the end of the world as we know it, and This Author, who freely admits she would not know heads from tails in such a world, would be forced to resign her post on the spot.

LADY WHISTLEDOWN'S SOCIETY PAPERS
13 JUNE 1817

Yellow, Mrs. Featherington declared, was a *happy* color and a *happy* girl would snare a husband.

Penelope decided then and there that it was best not to try to understand the workings of her mother's mind.

"I've spent my life forgetting things, not saying them, never telling anyone what I really want."

It was the three elder Bridgerton brothers: Anthony, Benedict, and Colin. They were having one of those conversations that men have, the kind in which they grumble a lot and poke fun at each other. Penelope had always liked to watch the Bridgertons interact in this manner; they were such a *family*.

Penelope could see them through the open front door, but she couldn't hear what they were saying until she'd reached the threshold. And in a testament to the bad timing that had plagued her throughout her life, the first voice she heard was Colin's, and the words were not kind.

"*. . . and I am certainly not going to marry Penelope Featherington!*"

"Oh!" The word slipped over her lips before she could even think, the squeal of it piercing the air like an off-key whistle.

The three Bridgerton men turned to face her with identical horrified faces, and Penelope knew that she had just entered into what would certainly be the most awful five minutes of her life.

She said nothing for what seemed like an eternity, and then, finally, with a dignity she never dreamed she possessed, she looked straight at Colin and said, "I never asked you to marry me."

THE VISCOUNT WHO LOVED ME

"I have rarely known Lady Whistledown to be incorrect," Kate said.

Penelope just shrugged and then looked down at her gown with disgust. "She certainly is never incorrect about *me*."

"Of course most of us still never lack for a dance partner," Cressida said, "but I do feel for poor Penelope when I see her sitting with the dowagers."

"The dowagers," Penelope ground out, "are often the only people in the room with a modicum of intelligence."

"If you want a new direction for your life," Penelope said, "then for heaven's sake, just pick something out and do it. The world is your oyster, Colin. You're young, wealthy, and you're a *man*." Penelope's voice turned bitter, resentful. "You can do anything you want."

He scowled, which didn't surprise her. When people were convinced they had problems, the last thing they wanted to hear was a simple, straightforward solution.

"It's not that simple," he said.

"It's exactly that simple."

She stood, smoothing out her skirts in an awkward, defensive gesture. "Next time you want to complain about the trials and tribulations of universal adoration, try being an on-the-shelf spinster for a day. See how that feels and then let me know what you want to complain about."

And then, while Colin was still sprawled on the sofa, gaping at her as if she were some bizarre creature with three heads, twelve fingers, and a tail, she swept out of the room.

It was, she thought as she descended the outer steps to Bruton Street, quite the most splendid exit of her existence.

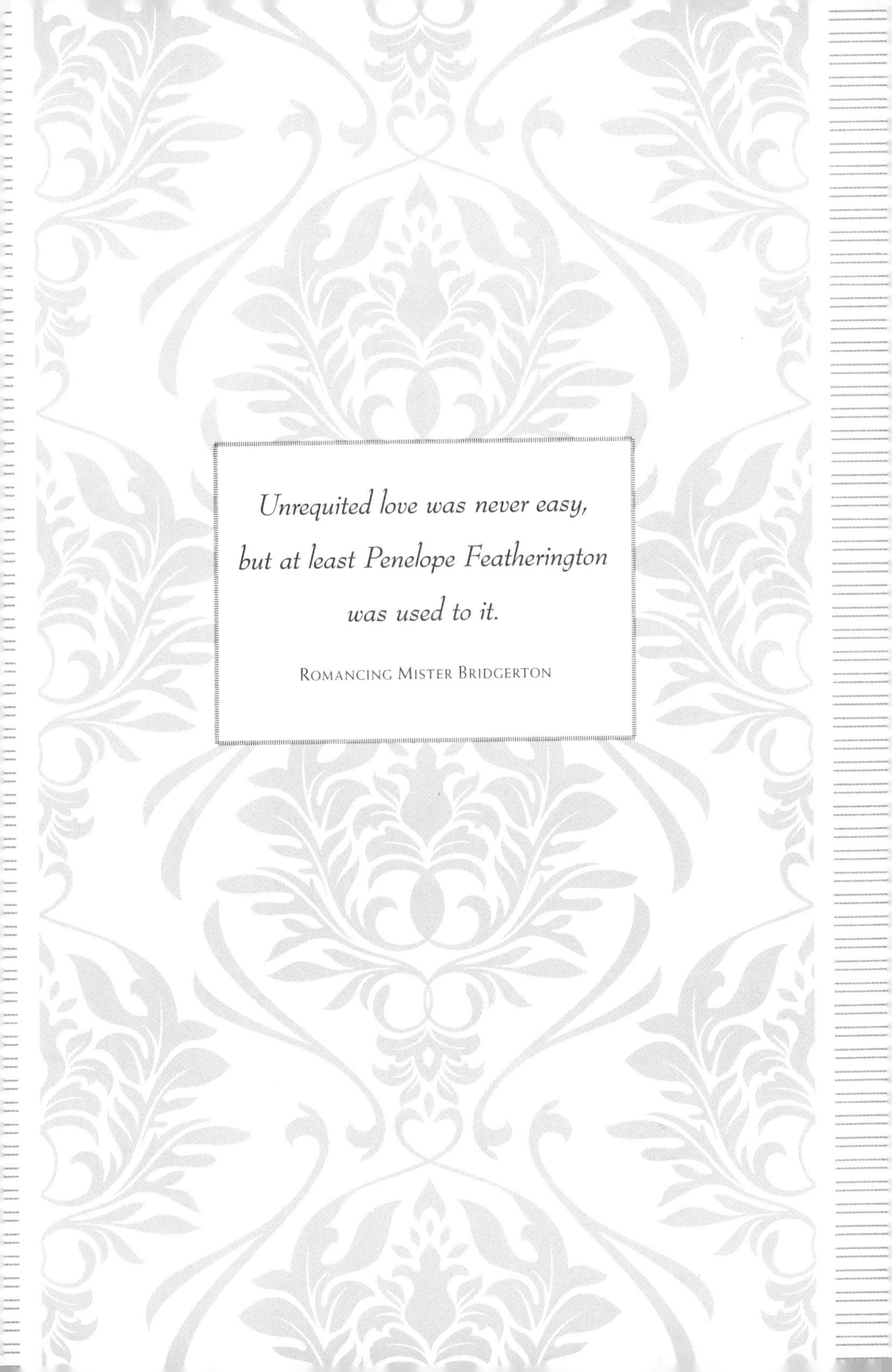

Unrequited love was never easy,

but at least Penelope Featherington

was used to it.

ROMANCING MISTER BRIDGERTON

"Happy endings are all I can do," she whispered. "I wouldn't know how to write anything else."

ROMANCING MISTER BRIDGERTON

ROMANCING MISTER BRIDGERTON

"Isn't it nice," Lady Danbury said, leaning in so that only Penelope could hear her words, "to discover that we're not exactly what we thought we were?"

And then she walked away, leaving Penelope wondering if maybe she wasn't quite what she'd thought she was.

Maybe—just maybe—she was something a little bit more.

"There's more to me than you think, Colin," she said. And then, in a quieter tone of voice, she added, "There's more to me than *I* used to think."

She always remembered the days of the week.

She'd met Colin on a Monday.

She'd kissed him on a Friday.

Twelve years later.

She sighed. It seemed fairly pathetic.

"Suppose I told everyone that I had seduced you."

Penelope grew very, very still.

"You would be ruined forever," Colin continued, crouching down near the edge of the sofa so that they were more on the same level. "It wouldn't matter that we had never even kissed. *That*, my dear Penelope, is the power of the word."

There are moments in a woman's life when her heart flips in her chest, when the world suddenly seems uncommonly pink and perfect, when a symphony can be heard in the tinkle of a doorbell.

It was the sort of kiss that enveloped her, from her head to her toes, from the way his teeth nibbled her lips, to his hands, squeezing her bottom and sliding across her back. It was the sort of kiss that could easily have turned her knees to water and led her to swoon on the sofa and allow him to do anything to her, the more wicked the better, even though they were mere yards away from over five hundred members of the *ton*, except—

"Colin!" she exclaimed, somehow breaking her mouth free of his.

"Shush."

"Colin, you have to stop!"

He looked like a lost puppy. "Must I?"

"Yes, you must."

"I suppose you're going to say it's because of all the people just next door."

"No, although that's a very good reason to consider restraint."

"To consider and then reject, perhaps?" he asked hopefully.

She had been born for this man, and she'd spent so many years trying to accept the fact that he had been born for someone else.

To be proven wrong was the most exquisite pleasure imaginable.

"I wouldn't have missed this for the world," Lady Danbury said. "Heh heh heh. All these fools, trying to figure out what you did to get Colin Bridgerton to marry you, when all you really did was be yourself."

PENELOPE, ACCORDING TO HER FAMIILY . . .

"Penelope never forgets a face."

ELOISE, *An Offer From a Gentleman*

"I've always liked her. More brains than the rest of her family put together."

LADY DANBURY, *Romancing Mister Bridgerton*

"There is no one I'd rather have as a sister. Well, aside from the ones I already have, of course."

ELOISE, *Romancing Mister Bridgerton*

"I know that many of you were surprised when
I asked Penelope Featherington to be my wife.
I was surprised myself."
A few unkind titters wafted through the air, but
Penelope held herself perfectly still, completely proud.
Colin would say the right thing. She knew he would.
Colin always said the right thing.
"I wasn't surprised that I had fallen in love with her,"
he said pointedly, giving the crowd a look that
dared them to comment, "but rather that it
had taken so long.
"I've known her for so many years, you see,"
he continued, his voice softening, "and somehow
I'd never taken the time to look inside, to see the
beautiful, brilliant, witty woman she'd become."

Romancing Mister Bridgerton

6

DAPHNE

Marriage, it seems, has not changed everything about the former Miss Daphne Bridgerton. While she has deftly transitioned from debutante to duchess, she is still a lady who grew up with four brothers, three of them her elder (and by next year, This Author is sure, all four of them taller). While the duchess, a former diamond of the first water, is all amiability and grace, there is much to her comportment that can only be explained by having grown up in a household so heavily populated by the males of our species. Consider the following:

At last season's house party at Aubrey Hall, after what was reported to be a lively game of Pall Mall in which the duchess's younger sister Eloise did not compete (apparently not for lack of trying, This Author was told), said sister recounted to a gaggle of rapt listeners that at a family gathering at Aubrey Hall the previous winter, the Duchess of Hastings not only partook in a lively snowball throwing competition, but she bested all of her participating brothers. The competition was judged by aim, not by distance, and This Author cannot help but think that the duchess's prowess was in part fueled by the fact that the target was Mr. Colin Bridgerton, who drew the season's short straw. (It should be noted that Eloise Bridgerton claims to have better aim than all her siblings. It should also be noted that according to several people with direct knowledge of the annual event, she has never drawn the short straw.)

But back to our fair duchess . . . At the Mottram ball last week, Mr. Harry Valentine gallantly saved one of the Smythe-Smith girls from crashing into the lemonade table following an unfortunate turn of events that included a small dog, a large clock, and Lady Danbury's cane. The duchess had barely recovered from being swept out of the way of the splintering glass by her gallant husband when she rushed over to Mr. Valentine to tend to his newly wounded hand. When complimented on her superior nursing skills and overall lack of squeamishness, the duchess did not so much as look away from her ministrations when she replied, "Four brothers. I have done this before."

It does make one wonder if there is anything the Duchess of Hastings cannot do.

"I want a husband. I want a family. It's not so silly when you think about it. I'm fourth of eight children. All I know are large families. I shouldn't know how to exist outside of one."

❁

"I knew nothing but love and devotion when I was growing up. Trust me, it makes everything easier."

❁

"I could do a great deal worse than follow your example, Mother," she murmured.

"Why Daphne," Violet said, her eyes growing watery, "what a lovely thing to say."

Daphne twirled a lock of her chestnut hair around her finger, and grinned, letting the sentimental moment melt into a more teasing one. "I'm happy to follow in your footsteps when it comes to marriage and children, Mother, just so long as I don't have to have *eight*."

Were you at Lady Danbury's ball last night? If not, shame on you. You missed witnessing quite the most remarkable coup of the season. It was clear to all partygoers, and especially to This Author, that Miss Daphne Bridgerton has captured the interest of the newly returned to England Duke of Hastings.

LADY WHISTLEDOWN'S SOCIETY PAPERS
30 APRIL 1813

THE VISCOUNT WHO LOVED ME

"We Bridgertons are a bloodthirsty lot, but we do like to follow tradition."

"We have no sense of sportsmanship when it comes to Pall Mall. When a Bridgerton picks up a mallet, we become the worst sorts of cheaters and liars. Truly, the game is less about winning than making sure the other players lose."

THE DUKE AND I

Daphne Bridgerton might be a marriageable female and thus a disaster waiting to happen for any man in his position, but she was certainly a good sport.

She was, it occurred to Simon in a rather bizarre moment of clarity, the sort of person he'd probably call friend if she were a man.

"Don't you have somewhere else to be?" Daphne asked pointedly.

Colin shrugged. "Not really."

“Didn’t,” she asked through clenched teeth, “you just tell me you promised a dance to Prudence Featherington?”

“Gads, no. You must have misheard.”

“Perhaps Mother is looking for you, then. In fact, I’m certain I hear her calling your name.”

Colin grinned at her discomfort. “You’re not supposed to be so obvious,” he said in a stage whisper, purposely loud enough for Simon to hear. “He’ll figure out that you like him.”

Simon’s entire body jerked with barely contained mirth.

“It’s not his company I’m trying to secure,” Daphne said acidly, “it’s yours I’m trying to avoid.”

Men, she thought with disgust, were interested only in those women who terrified them.

“Most people find me the soul of kindness and amiability.”

“Most people,” Simon said bluntly, “are fools.”

Daphne cocked her head to the side, obviously pondering his words. “I’m afraid I have to agree with you, much as it pains me.”

Simon bit back a smile. “It pains you to agree with me, or that most people are fools?”

“Both.” She grinned again—a wide, enchanting smile that did odd things to his brain. “But mostly the former.”

THE DUKE of Hastings was espied yet again with Miss Bridgerton. (That is Miss Daphne Bridgerton, for those of you who, like This Author, find it difficult to differentiate between the multitudes of Bridgerton offspring.) It has been some time since This Author has seen a couple so obviously devoted to one another.

LADY WHISTLEDOWN'S SOCIETY PAPERS
14 MAY 1813

"A rake's humor has its basis in cruelty. He needs a victim, for he cannot imagine ever laughing at himself."

And she thought—what if she kissed him? What if she pulled him into the garden and tilted her head up and felt his lips touch hers? Would he realize how much she loved him? How much he could grow to love her? And maybe—just maybe he'd realize how happy she made him.

She tried to say something witty; she tried to say something seductive. But her bravado failed her at the last moment. She'd never been kissed before, and now that she had all but invited him to be the first, she didn't know what to do.

"I've always known that I wasn't the sort of woman men dream of, but I never thought anyone would prefer death to marriage with me."

“All I want is you,” she whispered. “I don’t need the world, just your love. And maybe,” she added with a wry smile, “for you to take off your boots.”

“Did you know I have always suspected that men were idiots,” Daphne ground out, “but I was never positive until today.”

IT’S IN HIS KISS

“I cannot feel like a duchess in my mother’s sitting room.”

“What do you feel like, then?” Gareth asked.

“Hmmm.” She took a sip of her tea. “Just Daphne Bridgerton, I suppose. It’s difficult to shed the surname in this clan. In spirit, that is.”

“I hope that is a compliment,” Lady Bridgerton remarked.

Daphne just smiled at her mother. “I shall never escape you, I’m afraid.” She turned to Gareth. “There is nothing like one’s family to make one feel like one has never grown up.”

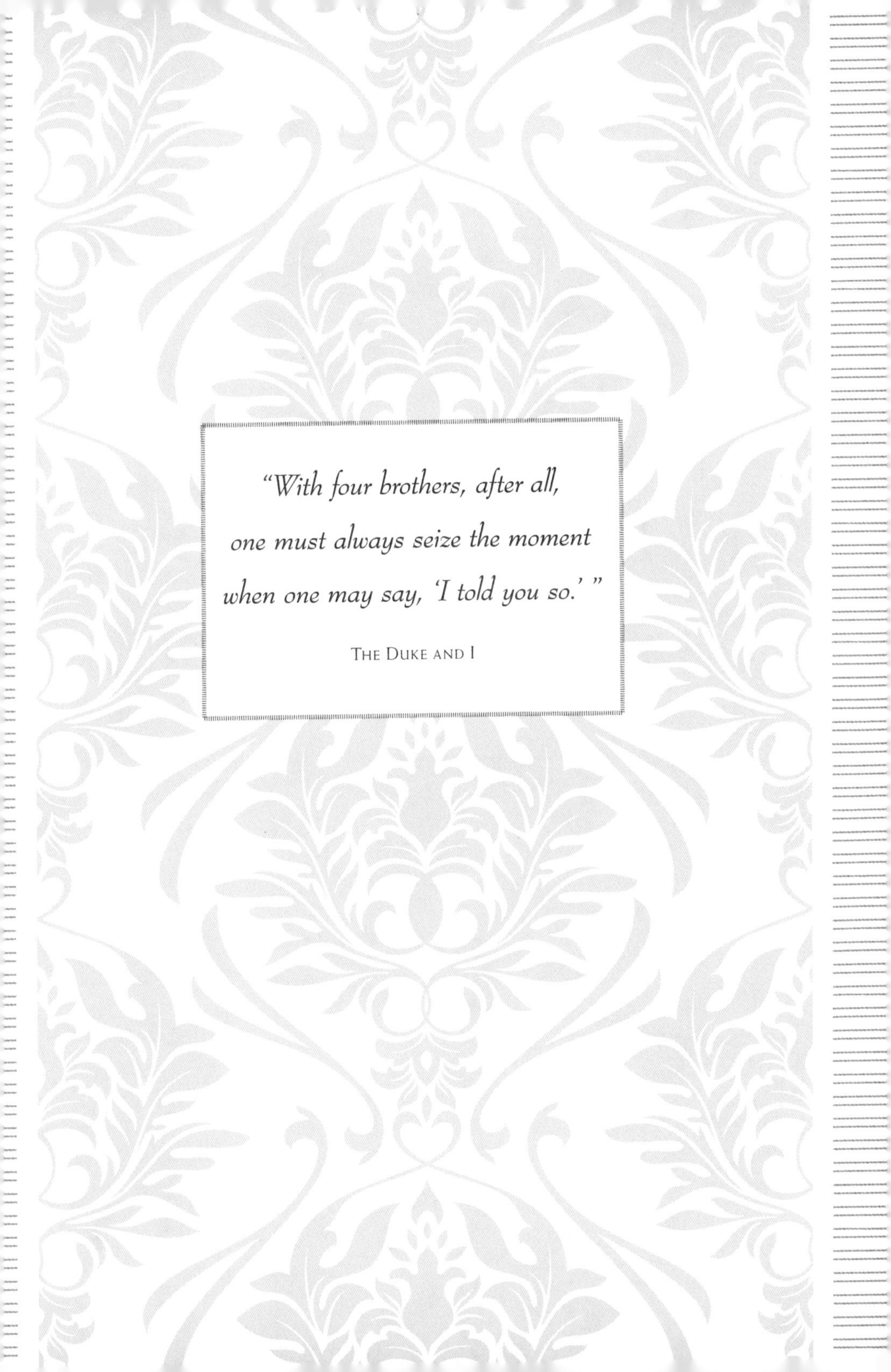
"With four brothers, after all,
one must always seize the moment
when one may say, 'I told you so.' "
The Duke and I

"I have long since learned that men positively yearn to be considered rakes."

The Duke and I

DAPHNE, ACCORDING TO HER FAMILY . . .

"I blame everything on Daphne.
It makes my life much easier."

COLIN, *The Viscount Who Loved Me*

Eloise supposed she should have talked to Daphne, but every time she went to see her, her elder sister was so bloody *happy*, so blissfully in love with her husband and her life as mother to her brood of four. How could someone like that possibly offer useful advice to one in Eloise's position?

To Sir Phillip, With Love

"Daphne's the exception that proves the rule.
You'll like her immensely."

ANTHONY, *The Duke and I*

7

SIMON

The Duke of Hastings is a *most* handsome man. And if Miss Daphne Bridgerton looks like confection on his arm, what does that make the dashing duke? A tasty snack, Dear Reader. Positively delicious. Feast on this tidbit that did cross This Author's ears following the Mottram Ball:

Two society matrons, one a Lady, one a widow, each with a glass of something spirited and sparkling in her hand, dipped their fluted cups at the duke in what can only be inferred as genuine appreciation as he passed. One then *mmm-mmm*ed as if she'd just sipped chocolate for the first time, and the other made a concurring nonverbal noise that was almost, dare I say it (yes, I will): *salacious*.

But has he more hair than wit? Negative, Dear Reader.

The duke is not one for idle conversation, nor does he speak often of his past, but This Author has it on the best authority that he took a first in Mathematics at Oxford. Which begs the question: Will Miss Daphne Bridgerton come in first when the Duke decides upon a Duchess?

LADY WHISTLEDOWN'S SOCIETY PAPERS, 1813

THE DUKE AND I

The birth of Simon Arthur Henry Fitzranulph Basset, Earl Clyvedon, was met with great celebration. Church bells rang for hours, champagne flowed freely through the gargantuan castle that the newborn would call home, and the entire village of Clyvedon quit work to partake of the feast and holiday ordered by the young earl's father.

"This," the baker said to the blacksmith, "is no ordinary baby."

"It's damned fine to have you back, Clyvedon," Anthony said once they'd settled in at their table at White's. "Oh, but I suppose you'll insist I call you Hastings now."

"No," Simon said rather emphatically. "Hastings will always be my father. He never answered to anything else." He paused. "I'll assume his title if I must, but I won't be called by his name."

"If you must?" Anthony's eyes widened slightly. "Most men would not sound quite so resigned about the prospect of a dukedom."

Simon raked a hand through his dark hair. He knew he was supposed to cherish his birthright and display unwavering pride in the Basset family's illustrious history, but the truth was it all made him sick inside. He'd spent his entire life not living up to his father's expectations; it seemed ridiculous now to try to live up to his name. "It's a damned burden is what it is."

IT HAS been reported to This Author that the Duke of Hastings mentioned no fewer than six times yestereve that he has no plans to marry. If his intention was to discourage the Ambitious Mamas, he made a grave error in judgment. They will simply view his remarks as the greatest of challenges.

LADY WHISTLEDOWN'S SOCIETY PAPERS
30 APRIL 1813

If he couldn't be the son his father wanted, then by God, he'd be the *exact opposite* . . .

"Prudence is quite accomplished on the pianoforte," Mrs. Featherington said.

Simon noted the oldest girl's pained expression and quickly decided never to attend a musicale chez Featherington.

"And my darling Phillipa is an expert watercolorist."

Phillipa beamed.

"And Penelope?" some devil inside Simon forced him to ask.

Mrs. Featherington shot a panicked look at her youngest daughter, who appeared to be quite miserable. Penelope was not terribly attractive, and her somewhat pudgy figure was not improved by her mother's choice of attire for her. But she seemed to have kind eyes.

"Penelope?" Mrs. Featherington echoed, her voice a touch shrill. "Penelope is . . . ah . . . well, she's Penelope!" Her mouth wobbled into a patently false grin.

Penelope looked as if she wanted to dive under a rug. Simon decided that if he was forced to dance, he'd ask Penelope.

It was those eyes as much as anything that had earned him his reputation as a man to be reckoned with. When he stared at a person, clear and unwavering, men grew uncomfortable. Women positively shivered.

⁂

"I think I know what your mother would say."

Daphne looked a little befuddled by his onslaught, but still she managed a rather defiant, "Oh?"

Simon nodded slowly, and he touched one finger to her chin. "She'd tell you to be very, very afraid."

There was a moment of utter silence, and then Daphne's eyes grew very wide. Her lips tightened, as if she were keeping something inside, and then her shoulders rose slightly, and then . . .

And then she laughed. Right in his face.

"Oh, my goodness," she gasped. "Oh, that was funny."

Simon was not amused.

"I'm sorry." This was said between laughs. "Oh, I'm sorry, but really, you shouldn't be so melodramatic. It doesn't suit you."

Simon paused, rather irritated that this slip of a girl had shown such disrespect for his authority. There were advantages to being considered a dangerous man, and being able to cow young maidens was supposed to be one of them.

"Well, actually, it does suit you, I ought to admit," she added, still grinning at his expense. "You looked quite dangerous. That was your intention, was it not?"

He still said nothing, so she said, "Of course it was. . . . Truly, I'm quite flattered you thought me worthy of such a magnificent display of dukish rakishness." She grinned, her smile wide and unfeigned. "Or do you prefer rakish dukishness?"

A DUEL, a duel, a duel. Is there anything more exciting, more romantic . . . or more utterly moronic?

LADY WHISTLEDOWN'S SOCIETY PAPERS
19 MAY 1813

"Those flowers are quite lovely," Daphne blurted out.

Simon regarded them lazily, rotating the bouquet with his wrist. "Yes, they are, aren't they?"

"I adore them."

"They're not for you."

Daphne choked on air.

Simon grinned. "They're for your mother."

Her mouth slowly opened in surprise, a short little gasp of air passing through her lips before she said, "Oh, you clever clever man."

Simon looked around. "Where is your brother? You're far too cheeky. Surely someone needs to take you in hand."

"Oh, I'm sure you'll be seeing more of Anthony," Daphne replied. "In fact I'm rather surprised he hasn't made an appearance yet. He was quite irate last night. I was forced to listen to a full hour's lecture on your many faults and sins."

"The sins are almost certainly exaggerated."

"And the faults?"

"Probably true," Simon admitted sheepishly.

That remark earned him another smile from Daphne. "Well, true or not," she said, "he thinks you're up to something."

"I *am* up to something."

Her head tilted sarcastically as her eyes rolled upward. "He thinks you're up to something nefarious."

"I'd like to be up to something nefarious," he muttered.

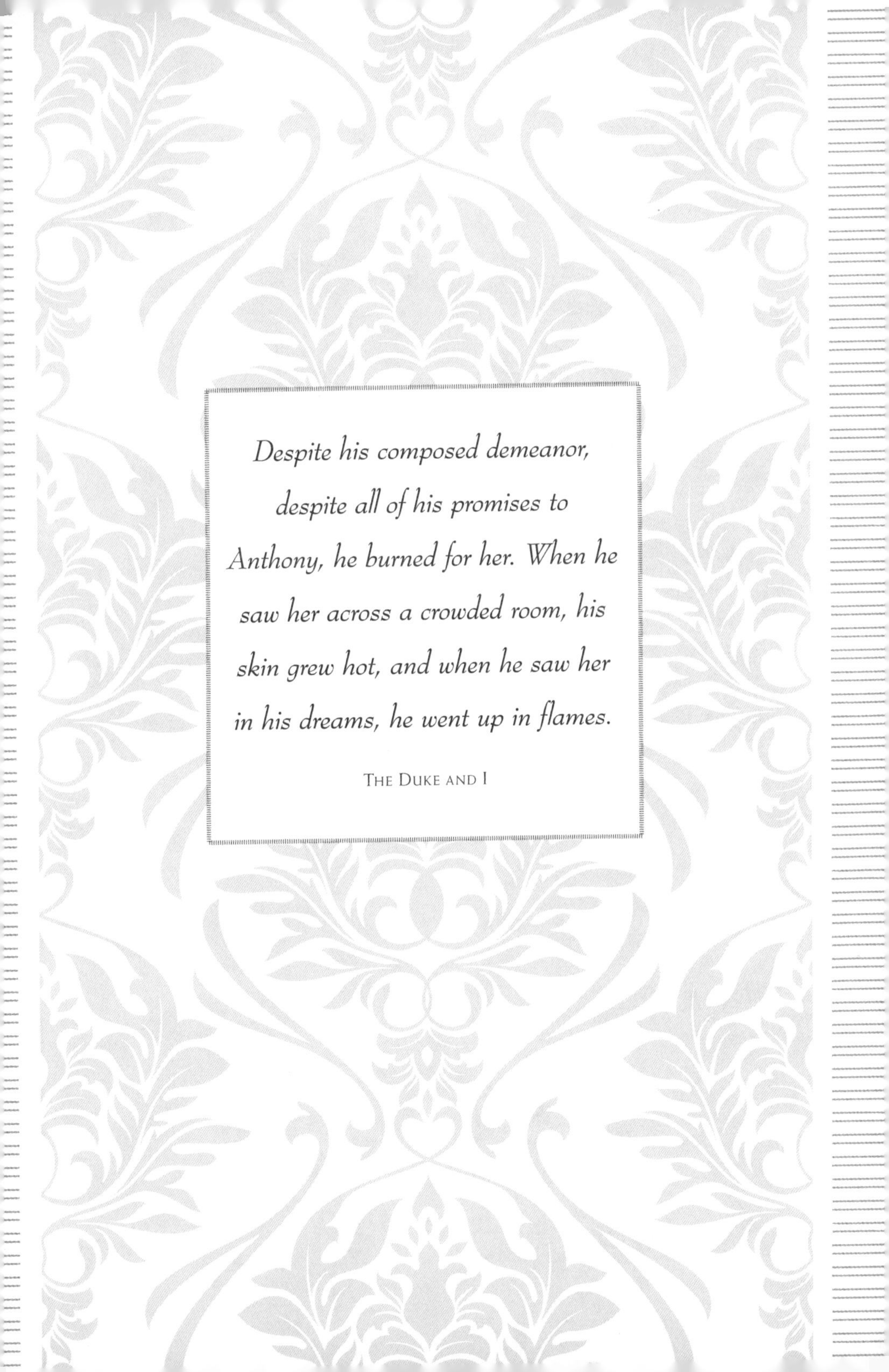

Despite his composed demeanor, despite all of his promises to Anthony, he burned for her. When he saw her across a crowded room, his skin grew hot, and when he saw her in his dreams, he went up in flames.

THE DUKE AND I

It is a truth universally acknowledged that a married man in possession of a good fortune must be in want of an heir.

LADY WHISTLEDOWN'S SOCIETY PAPERS
15 DECEMBER 1817

"I thought the primary rule of friendship was that one was not supposed to dally with one's friend's sister."

Simon smiled. "Ah, but I'm not dallying. I'm merely *pretending* to dally."

He whispered her name, touched her cheek.

Her eyes widened, lips parted.

And in the end, it was inevitable.

"It—it isn't you, Daphne. If it could be anyone it would be you. But marriage to me would destroy you. I could never give you what you want. You'd die a little every day, and it would kill me to watch."

"Didn't anyone tell you not to laugh at a man when he's trying to seduce you?"

"I didn't want any of this. I didn't want a wife, I didn't want a family, and I *definitely* didn't want to fall in love. But what I found . . . much to my dismay . . . was that it's quite impossible *not* to love you."

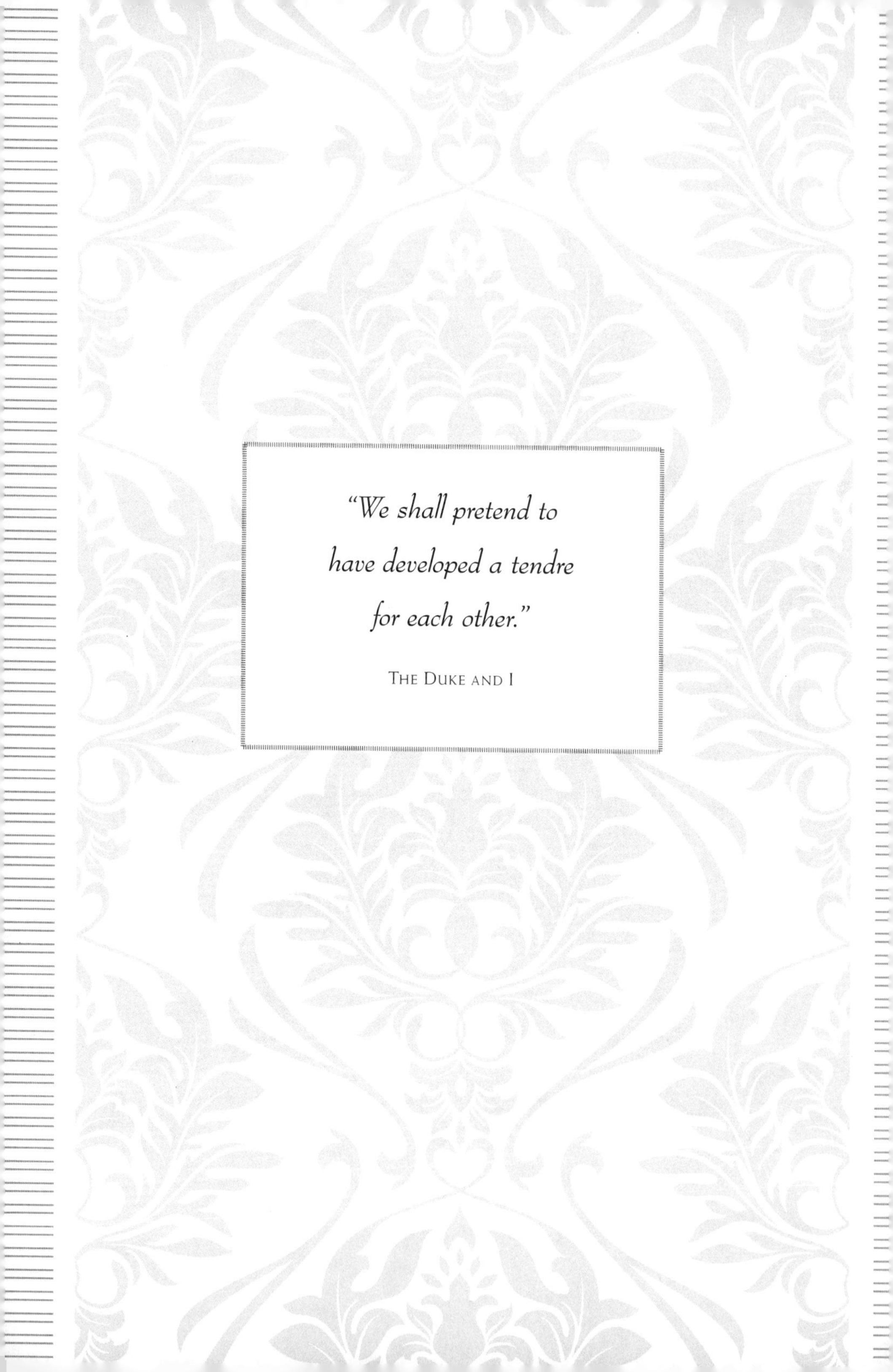

"We shall pretend to have developed a tendre for each other."

THE DUKE AND I

SIMON, ACCORDING TO HIS FAMILY . . .

"Anthony here has said such insulting things about you that I know we're sure to be great friends."

COLIN, *The Duke and I*

"You don't know," Anthony said, his voice low and nearly shaking with rage. "You don't know what he has done."

"No more than what you have done, I'm sure," Violet said slyly.

"Precisely!" Anthony roared. "Good God, I know exactly what is going on in his brain right now, and it has nothing to do with poetry and roses."

The Duke and I

"He was something of a hellion, if my memory serves. Always at odds with his father. But reputed to be quite brilliant. I'm fairly sure that Anthony said he took a first in mathematics. Which," Violet added with a maternal roll of her eyes, "is more than I can say for any of *my* children."

The Duke and I

8

ELOISE

Some years past, Lady Bridgerton remarked that Miss Eloise Bridgerton would make an excellent addition to the War Office. This tempting nugget of information is known to This Author because Miss Hyacinth Bridgerton happened to overhear, and she recounted the tale to Miss Felicity Featherington, who may or may not have repeated it in the presence of her mother. And as all London knows, once Mrs. Featherington sinks her claws into a bit of gossip, one might as well publish it in the *Sunday Times*.

Or here.

Nevertheless, one cannot help but wonder what prompted such a declaration. Lady Bridgerton was still Miss Sheffield at the time, and thus she could not have known that Eloise Bridgerton is an uncommonly good shot. While it is true that a lady's ability to join a hunt is certainly an asset, most men flatly do not appreciate a lady outshooting them, and indeed her brothers are no longer willing to compete against her in games of marksmanship.

(This Author finds this to be most badly done of them. Poor sports, indeed.)

Perhaps the former Miss Sheffield was instead referring to Miss Bridgerton's sharp wit and an acute attention to detail, both of which are now legendary. Indeed, more than one member of society has speculated that she could be Lady Whistledown.

She is not. This Author assures you. And This Author would be in a position to know.

LADY WHISTLEDOWN'S SOCIETY PAPERS, 1822

AN OFFER FROM A GENTLEMAN

"I know everything. You should know that by now."

"Just because we of the female gender are not allowed to study at places like Eton and Cambridge doesn't mean our educations are any less precious," Eloise ranted, completely ignoring her brother's weak "I know."

"Furthermore—" she carried on.

Benedict sagged against the wall.

"—I am of the opinion that the reason we are *not* allowed access is that if we *were*, we would trounce you men in all subjects!"

ROMANCING MISTER BRIDGERTON

When Eloise wanted something, she didn't stop until she had it firmly in her grasp. It wasn't about money, or greed, or material goods. With her it was about knowledge. She liked knowing things, and she'd needle and needle and needle until you'd told her exactly what she wanted to hear.

AN OFFER FROM A GENTLEMAN

"But," Eloise said, looking up with narrowed eyes, "that doesn't explain where you were all *week*."

"Has anyone ever told you that you are exceedingly nosy?" Benedict asked.

"Oh, all the time. Where were you?"

"And persistent, too."

"It's the only way to be."

TO SIR PHILLIP, WITH LOVE

. . . you will see why I could not accept his suit. He was too churlish by half and positively possessed of a foul temper. I should like to marry someone gracious and considerate, who treats me like a queen. Or at the very least, a princess. Surely that is not too much to ask.

FROM ELOISE BRIDGERTON TO HER DEAR FRIEND PENELOPE FEATHERINGTON, SENT BY MESSENGER AFTER ELOISE RECEIVED HER FIRST PROPOSAL OF MARRIAGE

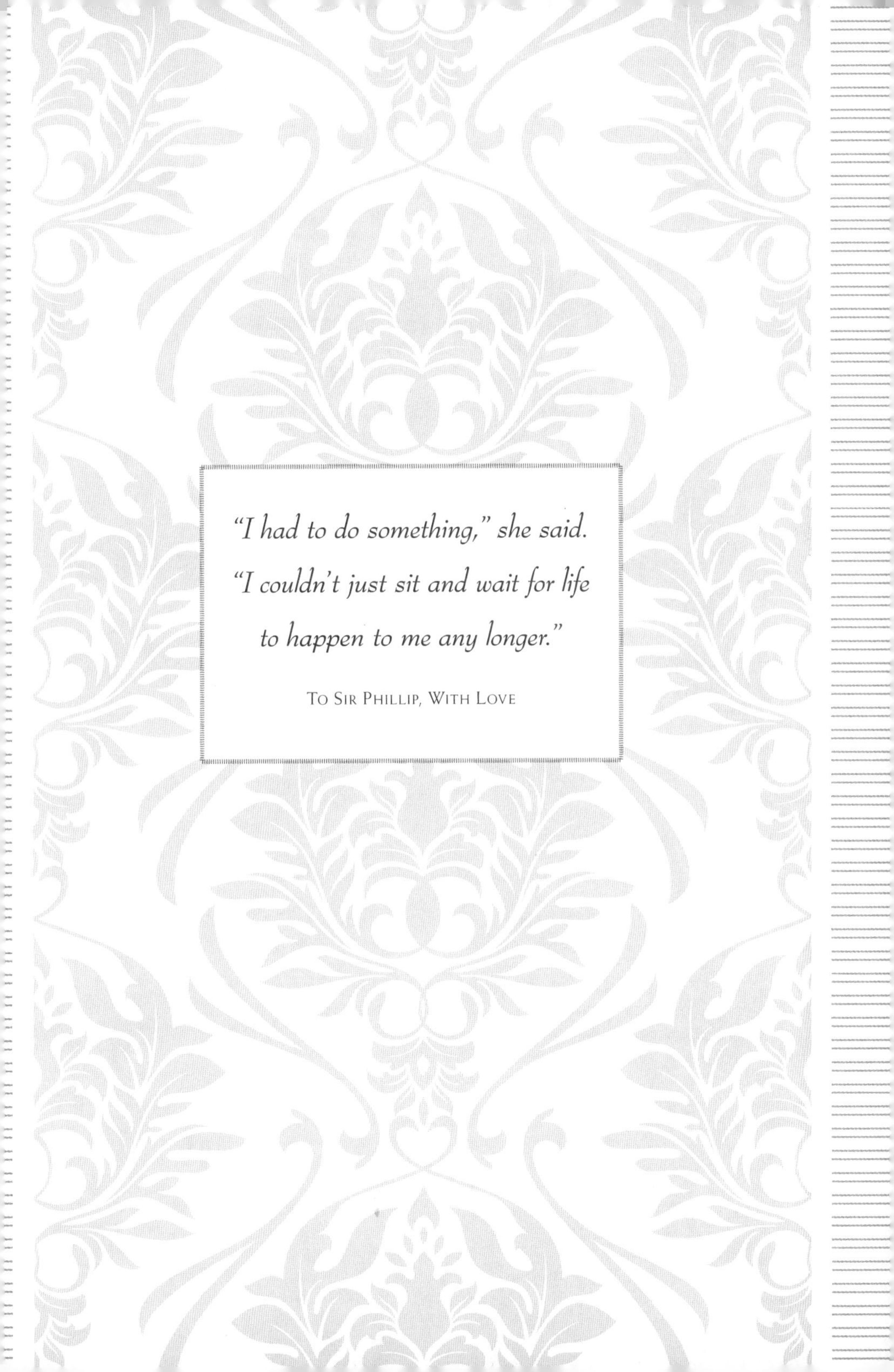
"I had to do something," she said. "I couldn't just sit and wait for life to happen to me any longer."
To Sir Phillip, With Love

Men. The day they learned to admit to a mistake was the day they became women.

To Sir Phillip, With Love

ROMANCING MISTER BRIDGERTON

"I'm perfectly comfortable as an old maid. . . . I'd much rather be a spinster than be married to a bore."

WHEN HE WAS WICKED

"You should go and talk to him," Eloise said, nudging Francesca with her elbow.

"Why on earth?"

"Because he's *here*."

"So are a hundred other men," Francesca replied, "all of whom I'd rather marry."

"I only see three I'd even consider promising to obey," Eloise muttered, "and I'm not even certain about them."

Hyacinth shrugged, jabbing a needle into her extremely untidy embroidery. "People still speak of him," she said carelessly. "The ladies swoon like idiots at the mere mention of his name, if you must know."

"There's no other way to swoon," put in Eloise.

"You should read a book, too, Eloise," Benedict suggested. "They're very improving."

"I don't need any improving," she shot back. "Give me a gun."

"I'm not giving you a gun," Benedict retorted. "We don't have enough to go around."

"We can share," Eloise ground out. "Have you ever tried sharing? It's very improving."

"You're very impatient," Violet said, facing the door. "You always have been."

"I know," Eloise said, wondering if this was a scolding, and if so, *why* was her mother choosing to do it now?

"I always loved that about you," Violet said. "I always loved everything about you, of course, but for some reason I always found your impatience especially charming. It was never because you wanted *more*, it was because you wanted everything."

Eloise wasn't so sure that sounded like such a good trait.

"You wanted everything for everyone, and you wanted to know it all and learn it all, and . . ."

For a moment Eloise thought her mother might be done, but then Violet turned around and added, "You've never been satisfied with second-best, and that's good, Eloise. I'm glad you never married any of those men who proposed in London. None of them would have made you happy. Content, maybe, but not happy."

Eloise felt her eyes widen with surprise.

"But don't let your impatience become all that you are," Violet said softly. "Because it isn't, you know. There's a great deal more to you, but I think sometimes you forget that."

And then she told him everything. All about the marriage proposals she'd received, and the ones Penelope hadn't, and the plans they'd jokingly made to grow old and spinsterish together. And she told him how guilty she'd felt when Penelope and Colin had married, and she couldn't stop thinking about herself, and how alone she was.

She told him all that and more. She told him what was in her mind and what was in her heart, and she told him things she'd never told another soul. And it occurred to her that for a woman who opened her mouth every other second, there was an awful lot inside of her that she'd never shared.

And then, when she was done (and in truth, she didn't even realize she'd finished; she just kind of ran out of energy and dwindled off into silence), he reached out and took her hand.

"It's all right," he said.

And it was, she realized. It actually was.

She didn't need someone perfect. She just needed someone perfect for her.

She loved the way he smiled, slightly lopsided, a little boyish, and with a little lilt of surprise, as if he couldn't quite believe in his own happiness.

She loved the way he looked at her, as if she were the most beautiful woman in the world when she knew, quite patently, that she was not.

She loved the way he actually listened to what she had to say, and the way he didn't allow her to cow him. She even loved the way he told her she talked too much, because he almost always did it with a smile, and because, of course, it was true.

And she loved the way he still listened to her, even after he told her she talked too much.

She loved the way he loved his children.

She loved his honor, his honesty, and his sly sense of humor.

And she loved the way she fit into his life, and the way he fit into hers.

It was comfortable. It was right.

And this, she finally realized, was where she belonged.

There is so much I hope to teach you, little one. I hope that I may do so by example, but I feel the need to put the words to paper as well. It is a quirk of mine, one which I expect you will recognize and find amusing by the time you read this letter.

Be strong.

Be diligent.

Be conscientious. There is never anything to be gained by taking the easy road. (Unless, of course, the road is an easy one to begin with. Roads sometimes are. If that should be the case, do not forge a new, more difficult one. Only martyrs go out looking for trouble.)

Love your siblings. You have two already, and God willing, there will be more. Love them well, for they are your blood, and when you are unsure, or times are difficult, they will be the ones to stand by your side.

Laugh. Laugh out loud, and laugh often. And when circumstances call for silence, turn your laugh into a smile.

Don't settle. Know what you want and reach for it. And if you don't know what you want, be patient. The answers will come to you in time, and you may find that your heart's desire has been right under your nose all the while.

And remember, always remember that you have a mother and a father who love each other and love you.

I feel you growing restless. Your father is making strange gasping sounds and will surely lose his temper altogether if I do not move from my escritoire to my bed.

Welcome to the world, little one. We are all so delighted to make your acquaintance.

FROM ELOISE, LADY CRANE, TO HER DAUGHTER PENELOPE, UPON THE OCCASION OF HER BIRTH

ELOISE, ACCORDING TO HER FAMILY . . .

"*You* happen to life, Eloise," Anthony said. "You've always made your own decisions, always been in control. It might not always feel that way, but it's true."

To Sir Phillip, With Love

"That girl could get Napoleon to spill his secrets."

VIOLET, *An Offer From a Gentleman*

Francesca would have given her life for Eloise, of course, and there was certainly no other woman who knew more of her secrets and inner thoughts, but half the time she could have happily strangled her sister.

When He Was Wicked

There were *two* things about her that colored her every action—she liked to act quickly and she was tenacious. Penelope had once described her as akin to a dog with a bone. And Penelope had not been joking.

To Sir Phillip, With Love

9

FRANCESCA

Francesca Stirling, the Countess of Kilmartin, wore blue the other evening.

Not black, not gray or lavender, Dear Reader. Blue.

This can only mean one thing. And it's not the deflection uttered by her sister Miss Hyacinth Bridgerton: "Well, she *likes* the color blue." (Thank you, Hyacinth.)

Francesca Stirling, the widowed Countess of Kilmartin, is considering remarrying.

And lest anyone think this is too great an assumption to make based on the color of one's gown, Miss Eloise Bridgerton said it plain: The widowed countess is indeed entertaining the possibility of remarrying. But even she hinted that she'd been taken by surprise by her sister's intentions.

But this is par for the course for Lady Kilmartin, always the most reserved of the Bridgerton brood. It seems as if by the time This Author knows of something the third Bridgerton daughter has done, enough time has passed that it should be considered old news.

LADY WHISTLEDOWN'S SOCIETY PAPERS, 1824

"Mother has told you," fourteen-year-old Hyacinth said, "at least a *thousand* times—"

"A thousand times?" Francesca asked with arched brows.

"A hundred times," Hyacinth amended, shooting an annoyed look at her older sister, "that you do not have to bring your mending to tea."

Sophie suppressed a smile of her own. "I should feel very lazy if I did not."

"Well, I'm not going to bring my embroidery," Hyacinth announced, not that anyone had asked her to.

"Feeling lazy?" Francesca queried.

"Not in the least," Hyacinth returned.

Francesca turned to Sophie. "You're making Hyacinth feel lazy."

"I do not!" Hyacinth protested.

Lady Bridgerton sipped at her tea. "You *have* been working on the same piece of embroidery for quite some time, Hyacinth. Since February, if my memory serves."

"Her memory always serves," Francesca said to Sophie.

Hyacinth glared at Francesca, who smiled into her teacup.

Sophie coughed to cover a smile of her own. Francesca, who at twenty was merely one year younger than Eloise, had a sly, subversive sense of humor. Someday Hyacinth would be her match, but not yet.

WHEN HE WAS WICKED

She didn't like to be thwarted, and she certainly did not enjoy admitting that she might not be able to arrange her world—and the people inhabiting it—to her satisfaction.

TO SIR PHILLIP, WITH LOVE

"What did you say to Francesca?" Eloise asked.

"I beg your pardon?"

"Francesca," Eloise repeated, referring to her younger sister who had married six years earlier—and was tragically widowed two years after that. "What did you say to her when she married? You mentioned Daphne, but not Francesca."

Violet's blue eyes clouded, as they always did when she thought of her third daughter, widowed so young. "You know Francesca. I expect she could have told me a thing or two."

Eloise gasped.

"I don't mean it *that* way, of course," Violet hastened to add. . . . "But you know Francesca. She's so sly and knowing. I expect she bribed some poor housemaid into explaining it all to her years earlier."

Eloise nodded. She didn't want to tell her mother that she and Francesca had in fact pooled their pin money to bribe the housemaid. It had been worth every penny, however. Annie Mavel's explanation had been detailed and, Francesca had later informed her, absolutely correct.

SUCH A scurry on Bruton Street. The dowager Viscountess Bridgerton and her son Benedict Bridgerton were seen dashing out of her house Friday morning. Mr. Bridgerton practically threw his mother into a carriage, and they took off at breakneck speed. Francesca and Hyacinth Bridgerton were seen standing in the doorway, and This Author has it on the best authority that Francesca was heard to utter a very unladylike word.

LADY WHISTLEDOWN'S SOCIETY PAPERS
16 JUNE 1817

WHEN HE WAS WICKED

Francesca slathered more jam on her muffin. "I'm eating, Hyacinth."

Her youngest sister shrugged. "So am I, but it doesn't prevent me from carrying on an intelligent conversation."

"I'm going to kill her," Francesca said to no one in particular. Which was probably a good thing, as there was no one else present.

"Who are you talking to?" Hyacinth demanded.

"God," Francesca said baldly. "And I do believe I have been given divine leave to murder you."

"Hmmph," was Hyacinth's response. "If it was that easy, I'd have asked permission to eliminate half the *ton* years ago."

Francesca decided just then that not all of Hyacinth's statements required a rejoinder. In fact, few of them did.

Francesca didn't like to think of herself as a coward, but when her choices were that and fool, she chose coward. Gladly.

Francesca couldn't help but smile. "I do," she said softly. "I want a baby."

"I thought that you did."

"Why did you never ask me about it?"

Violet tilted her head to the side. "Why did you never ask me about why I never remarried?"

Francesca felt her lips part. She shouldn't have been so surprised by her mother's perceptiveness.

"If you had been Eloise, I think I would have said something," Violet added. "Or any of your sisters, for that matter. But you—" She smiled nostalgically. "You're not the same. You never have been. Even as a child you set yourself apart. And you needed your distance."

Impulsively, Francesca reached out and squeezed her mother's hand. "I love you, did you know that?"

Violet smiled. "I rather suspected it."

No one had ever told her how sad she'd be. Who would have *thought* to tell her? And even if someone had, even if her mother, who had also been widowed young, had explained the pain, how could she have understood?

It was one of those things that had to be experienced to be understood. And oh, how Francesca wished she didn't belong to this melancholy club.

"The fact of the matter," Kate continued, "is that most of humanity has more hair than wit. If you wish for people to be aware that you are on the Marriage Mart, you shall have to make it quite clear. Or rather, we shall have to make it clear for you."

Francesca had horrible visions of her female relatives, chasing down men until the poor fellows ran screaming for the doors.

ON THE WAY TO THE WEDDING

It was an odd location for a bench, facing nothing but a bunch of trees. But maybe that was the point. Turning one's back on the house—and its many inhabitants. Francesca had often said that after a day or two with the entire Bridgerton family, trees could be quite good company.

WHEN HE WAS WICKED

She'd never dreamed that Michael might have secrets from her. From *her*! Everyone else, maybe, but not her.

And it left her feeling rather off-balance and untidy. Almost as if someone had come up to Kilmartin House and shoved a pile of bricks under the south wall, setting the entire world at a drunken slant. No matter what she did, no matter what she thought, she still felt as if she were sliding. To where, she didn't know, and she didn't dare hazard a guess.

But the ground was most definitely no longer firm beneath her feet.

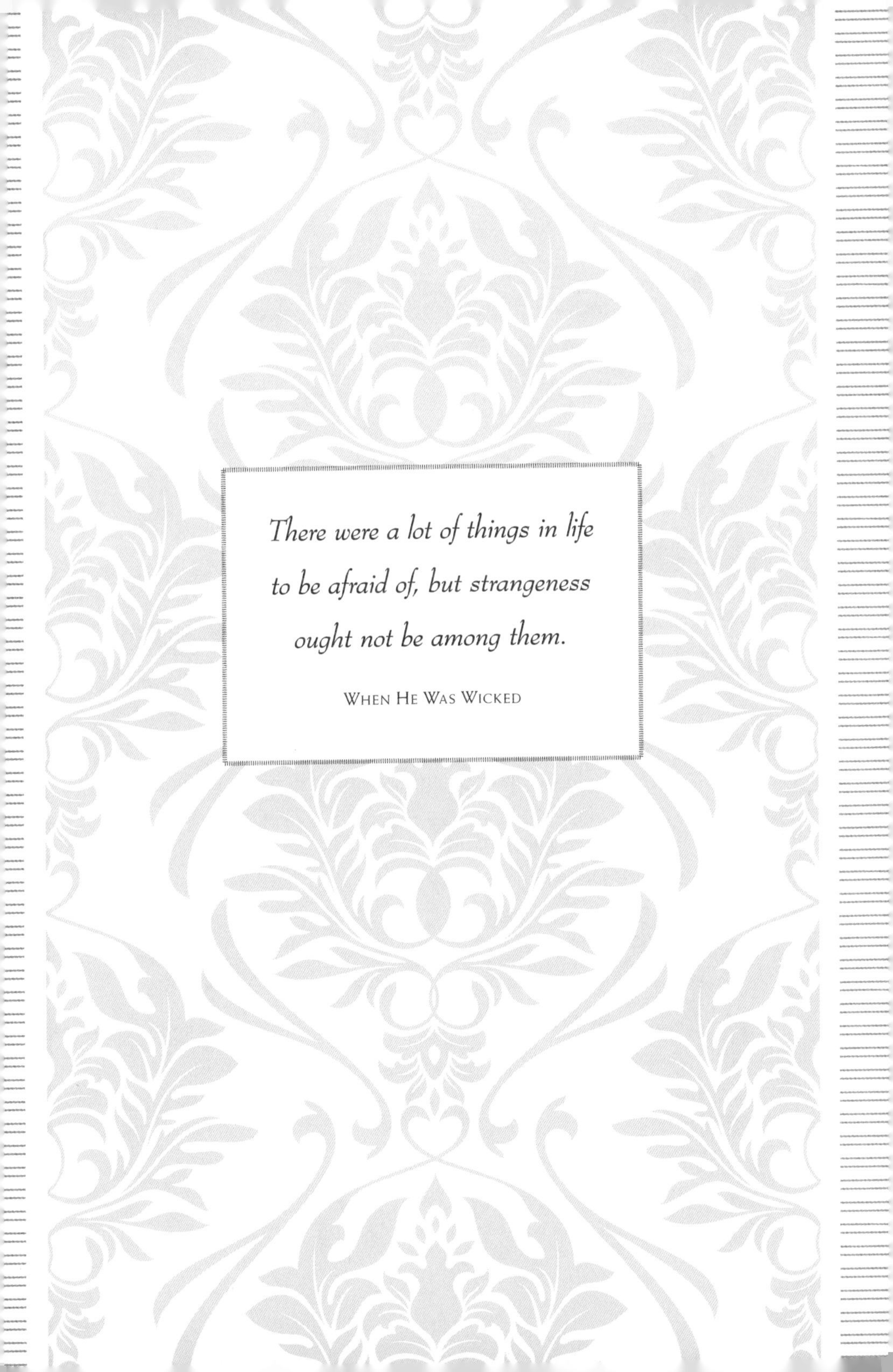

There were a lot of things in life to be afraid of, but strangeness ought not be among them.

When He Was Wicked

"I can't believe no one *told* me."

"You *have* been in Scotland."

"Still," Francesca said grumpily.

Michael just chuckled at her annoyance, drat the man.

"It's as if I don't exist," she said, irritated enough to shoot him her most ferocious glare.

"Oh, I wouldn't say—"

"Oh, yes," she said with great flair, "*Francesca.*"

"Frannie . . ." He sounded quite amused now.

"Has someone told Francesca?" she said, doing a rather fine group impression of her family. "Remember her? Sixth of eight? The one with the blue eyes?"

"Frannie, don't be daft."

"I'm not daft, I'm just ignored."

"I rather thought you liked being a bit removed from your family."

"Well, yes," she grumbled, "but that's beside the fact."

She loved Michael.

Not just as a friend, but as a husband and a lover. She loved him with the depth and intensity she'd felt for John. It was different, because they were different men, and she was different now, too, but it was also the same. It was the love of a woman for a man, and it filled every corner of her heart.

She was different. She'd always felt a little different from the rest of her family. She loved them fiercely, and would have laid down her life for any one of them, but even though she looked like a Bridgerton, on the inside she always felt like a bit of a changeling.

When He Was Wicked

FRANCESCA, ACCORDING TO HER FAMILY . . .

Eloise wanted her sisters. Not Hyacinth, who was barely one and twenty and knew nothing of men, but one of her married sisters. She wanted Daphne, who always knew what to say, or Francesca, who never said what one wanted to hear but always managed to eke out a smile nonetheless.

To Sir Phillip, With Love

. . . you would enjoy it here. Not the heat, I should think; no one seems to enjoy the heat. But the rest would enchant you. The colors, the spices, the scent of the air—they can place you in a strange, sensuous haze that is at turns unsettling and intoxicating. Most of all, I think you would enjoy the pleasure gardens. They are rather like our London parks, except far more green and lush, and full of the most remarkable flowers you have ever seen. You have always loved to be out among nature; this you would adore, I am quite sure of it.

FROM MICHAEL STIRLING (THE NEW EARL OF KILMARTIN) TO THE COUNTESS OF KILMARTIN, ONE MONTH AFTER HIS ARRIVAL IN INDIA

When He Was Wicked

. . . yes, of course. Francesca is a wonder. But you already knew that, didn't you?

FROM HELEN STIRLING TO HER SON, THE EARL OF KILMARTIN, TWO YEARS AND NINE MONTHS AFTER HIS DEPARTURE FOR INDIA

When He Was Wicked

10

GREGORY

Can men make debuts in society? If so, the youngest Bridgerton brother—that would be Gregory, for those of you living under rocks—made his Thursday last at the annual Danbury ball. Female hearts were predictably aflutter, as Bridgerton version G bears a strong resemblance to Bridgerton versions A, B, and C. Unlike A and B, however, G is unmarried and thus available, and unlike C, he is conveniently located within the boundaries of our great nation.

Where is Colin Bridgerton these days? Northern France? Southern Spain? The East Northeast of Saxony? This Author does not know.

But back to young Master Gregory. This Author fears that if the *ton* simply must have a Bridgerton brother on the social scene, it shall have to make do with the youngest. Will version G be up to the task? Judging from the reaction of every unmarried miss save for his sister Hyacinth, the answer is yes.

Unlike most men of his acquaintance, Gregory Bridgerton believed in true love.

He'd have to have been a fool not to.

Consider the following:

His eldest brother Anthony.

His eldest sister Daphne.

His other brothers Benedict and Colin, not to mention his sisters Eloise, Francesca, and (galling but true) Hyacinth, all of whom—all of whom—were quite happily besotted with their spouses.

For most men, such a state of affairs would produce nothing quite so much as bile, but for Gregory, who had been born with an uncommonly cheerful, if occasionally (according to his younger sister) annoying, spirit, it simply meant that he had no choice but to believe the obvious:

Love existed.

Gregory was, by all accounts, a fairly typical man about London, with a comfortable—although by no means extravagant—allowance, plenty of friends, and a level enough head to know when to quit a gaming table. He was considered a decent enough catch on the Marriage Mart, if not precisely the top selection (fourth sons never did command a great deal of attention), and he was always in demand when the society matrons needed an eligible man to even up the numbers at dinner parties.

"There is comfort in having a family, I think. It's a sense of . . . just *knowing*, I suppose. . . . I know that they are there," Gregory said, "that should I ever be in trouble, or even simply in need of a good conversation, I can always turn to them."

"I have a brother," Lucy said. "He delights in tormenting me."

Gregory offered her a grave nod. "That is what brothers are meant to do."

"Do you torment your sisters?"

"Mostly just the younger one."

"Because she's smaller."

"No, because she deserves it."

IT'S IN HIS KISS

"Well," Gregory said with an affected sigh, "you have my approval, at least."

"Why?" Hyacinth asked suspiciously.

"It would be an excellent match," he continued. "If nothing else, think of the children."

"What children?"

He grinned. "The lovely lithping children you could have together. Garethhhh and Hyathinthhhh. Hyathinth and Gareth. And the thublime Thinclair tots."

She shook her head. "How on earth Mother managed to give birth to seven perfectly normal children and one freak is beyond me."

"Thith way to the nurthery," Gregory laughed as she headed back into the room. "With the thcrumptious little Tharah and Thamuel Thinclair. Oh, yeth, and don't forget wee little Thuthannah!"

TO SIR PHILLIP, WITH LOVE

"I'm dropping out," Gregory muttered. "I haven't eaten breakfast yet."

"You'll have to ring for more," Colin told him. "I already finished it all."

Gregory let out an annoyed sigh. "It's a wonder I haven't starved," he grumbled, "younger brother that I am."

Colin shrugged. "You've got to be quick if you want to eat."

Anthony looked at the two of them with disgust. "Did the two of you grow up in an orphanage?"

"Men don't gossip.
We talk."
On the Way to the Wedding

ON THE WAY TO THE WEDDING

"I expect I'll join the clergy. . . . It's not as if I've many choices," Gregory said. And as the words emerged, he realized it was the first time he'd spoken them. It somehow made them more real, more permanent. "It's the military or the clergy," he continued, "and, well, it's got to be said—I'm a beastly bad shot."

"How fares your courtship?" Kate asked him.

Anthony's ears perked up. "Your courtship?" he echoed, his face assuming its usual *obey-me-I-am-the-viscount* expression. "Who is she?"

Gregory shot Kate an aggravated look. He had not shared his feelings with his brother. He wasn't sure why; surely in part because he hadn't actually *seen* much of Anthony in the past few days. But there was more. It just didn't seem like the sort of thing one wished to share with one's brother. Especially one who was considerably more father than brother.

Not to mention. . . . If he didn't succeed . . .

Well, he didn't particularly wish for his family to know.

But he would succeed. Why was he doubting himself? Even earlier, when Miss Watson was still treating him like a minor nuisance, he had been sure of the outcome. It made no sense that now—with their friendship growing—he should suddenly doubt himself.

Kate, predictably, ignored Gregory's irritation. "I just adore it when you don't know something," she said to her husband. "Especially when I do."

Anthony turned to Gregory. "You're sure you want to marry one of these?"

"Not that one precisely," Gregory answered. "Something rather like it, though."

This was everything he'd ever imagined love to be. Huge, sudden, and utterly exhilarating.

And somehow crushing at the same time.

It was a damned good thing men couldn't have children. Gregory took no shame in admitting that the human race would have died out generations earlier.

"I won't say a word," Hyacinth promised, waving her hand as if she had never spoken out of turn in her life.

Gregory let out a snort. "Oh, *please*."

"I won't," she protested. "I am superb with a secret as long as I *know* it is a secret."

"Ah, so what you mean, then, is that you possess no sense of discretion?"

Hyacinth narrowed her eyes.

Gregory lifted his brows.

"How *old* are you?" Violet interjected. "Goodness, the two of you haven't changed a bit since you were in leading strings. I half expect you to start pulling each other's hair right on the spot."

Gregory clamped his jaw into a line and stared resolutely ahead. There was nothing quite like a rebuke from one's mother to make one feel three feet tall.

His piss-poor marksmanship guaranteed that he couldn't hit anything that moved, and it was a damned good thing he wasn't responsible for acquiring his own food.

"Do you think it could possibly be different for different people? If you loved someone, truly and deeply, wouldn't it feel like . . . like *everything*?"

He believed in love.
Wasn't that the one thing that had
been a constant in his life?
He believed in love.
He believed in its power, in its
fundamental goodness, its rightness.
He revered it for its strength,
respected it for its rarity.
And he knew, right then, right
there, as she cried in his arms, that
he would dare anything for it.

ON THE WAY TO THE WEDDING

He sat on the opposite end of the bench and began to tear his bread into bits. When he had a good-sized handful, he tossed them all at once, then sat back to watch the ensuing frenzy of beaks and feathers.

Lucy, he noticed, was tossing her crumbs methodically, one after another, precisely three seconds apart.

He counted. How could he not?

"The flock has abandoned me," she said with a frown.

Gregory grinned as the last pigeon hopped to the feast of Bridgerton. He threw down another handful. "I always host the best parties."

He had never gone to his brothers for help, never begged them to extricate him from a tight spot. He was a relatively young man. He had drunk spirits, gambled, dallied with women.

But he had never drunk too much, or gambled more than he had, or, until the previous night, dallied with a woman who risked her reputation to be with him.

He had not sought responsibility, but neither had he chased trouble.

His brothers had always seen him as a boy. Even now, in his twenty-eighth year, he suspected they did not view him as quite fully grown. And so he did not ask for help. He did not place himself in any position where he might need it.

Until now.

❀

The odds were *extremely* against him. But Gregory had always been one to cheer for the underdog. And if there was any sense of justice in the world, any existential fairness floating through the air. . . . If *Do unto others* offered any sort of payback, surely he was due.

Love existed.

He knew that it did. And he would be damned if it did not exist for him.

GREGORY, ACCORDING TO HIS FAMILY . . .

Eloise turned to her brothers and motioned to each in turn, saying, "Anthony, Benedict, Colin, Gregory. These three," she added, motioning to A, B, and C, "are my elders. This one"—she waved dismissively at Gregory, "is an infant."

To Sir Phillip, With Love

"All I am trying to say is that you have never had to expend much of an effort to achieve your goals. Whether that is a result of your abilities or your goals, I am not certain."

VIOLET, *On the Way to the Wedding*

Violet sighed. "Hyacinth, I declare that you will be the death of me."

"No, I won't," Hyacinth replied. "Gregory will."

Romancing Mister Bridgerton

11

HYACINTH

Miss Hyacinth Bridgerton made her debut this week, and while she acquitted herself admirably, executing the most graceful curtsy when presented to the King, it did not escape This Author's note that her mother watched over her like the proverbial hawk, her expression vaguely queasy all the while.

It was almost as if Lady Bridgerton anticipated disaster.

LADY WHISTLEDOWN'S SOCIETY PAPERS, 1821

THE DUKE AND I

"You Bridgerton ladies are very demanding, did you know that?"

Hyacinth viewed him with a mixture of suspicion and glee. Suspicion finally won out. Her hands found their way to her little hips as she narrowed her eyes and asked, "Are you funning me?"

Simon smiled right at her. "What do you think?"

"I think you are."

"I think I'm lucky there aren't any puddles about."

Hyacinth pondered that for a moment. "If you decide to marry my sister—"

Daphne choked on a biscuit.

"—then you have my approval."

Simon choked on air.

"But if you don't," Hyacinth continued, smiling shyly, "then I'd be much obliged if you'd wait for me."

IT'S IN HIS KISS

"I used to think," Hyacinth said after a moment, "that the only thing that would have made my life better was a father."

Gareth said nothing.

"Whenever I was angry with my mother," she continued, still

standing by the door, "or with one of my brothers or sisters, I used to think—*If only I had a father. Everything would be perfect, and he would surely take my side.*" She looked up, and her lips were curved in an endearingly lopsided smile. "He wouldn't have done, of course, since I'm sure that most of the time I was in the wrong, but it gave me great comfort to think it."

"*Touché*, Miss Bridgerton."

Hyacinth sighed happily. "My three favorite words."

Violet took a sip of her tea. "I'm not certain you'd know the right sort of man for you if he arrived on our doorstep riding an elephant."

"I would think," Hyacinth replied, "the elephant would be a fairly good indication that I ought to look elsewhere."

No one seemed to actually dislike Hyacinth—there was a certain charm to her that kept her in everyone's good graces—but the consensus was that she was best in small doses. "Men don't like women who are more intelligent than they are," one of Gareth's shrewder friends had commented, "and Hyacinth Bridgerton isn't the sort to feign stupidity."

“I know that it is considered unseemly to display one’s emotions,” Violet said, “and certainly I would not suggest that you engage in anything that might be termed histrionic, but sometimes it does help to simply tell someone how you feel.”

Hyacinth looked up, meeting her mother’s gaze directly. “I rarely have difficulty telling people how I feel.”

“Tell me, Hyacinth,” Lady Danbury said, leaning forward, “how are your prospects these days?”

“You sound like my mother,” Hyacinth said sweetly.

“A compliment of the highest order,” Lady D tossed back. “I like your mother, and I hardly like anyone.”

“I’ll be sure to tell her.”

“Bah. She knows that already, and you’re avoiding the question.”

“My prospects,” Hyacinth replied, “as you so delicately put it, are the same as ever.”

“Such is the problem. You, my dear girl, need a husband.”

“Are you quite certain my mother isn’t hiding behind the curtains, feeding you lines?”

“See?” Lady Danbury said with a wide smile. “I *would* be good on the stage.”

Hyacinth just stared at her. “You have gone quite mad, did you know that?”

"Bah. I'm merely old enough to get away with speaking my mind. You'll enjoy it when you're my age, I promise."

"I enjoy it now," Hyacinth said.

"True," Lady Danbury conceded. "And it's probably why you're still unmarried."

ROMANCING MISTER BRIDGERTON

Violet sat next to Hyacinth across from Penelope and Eloise. "Do tell, Penelope, what did Colin mean when he instructed us to stick to you like glue?"

"I'm sure I don't know."

Violet's eyes narrowed, as if assessing her honesty. "He was quite emphatic. He underlined the word 'glue,' you know."

"He underlined it twice," Hyacinth added. "If his ink had been any darker, I'm sure I would have had to go out and slaughter a horse myself."

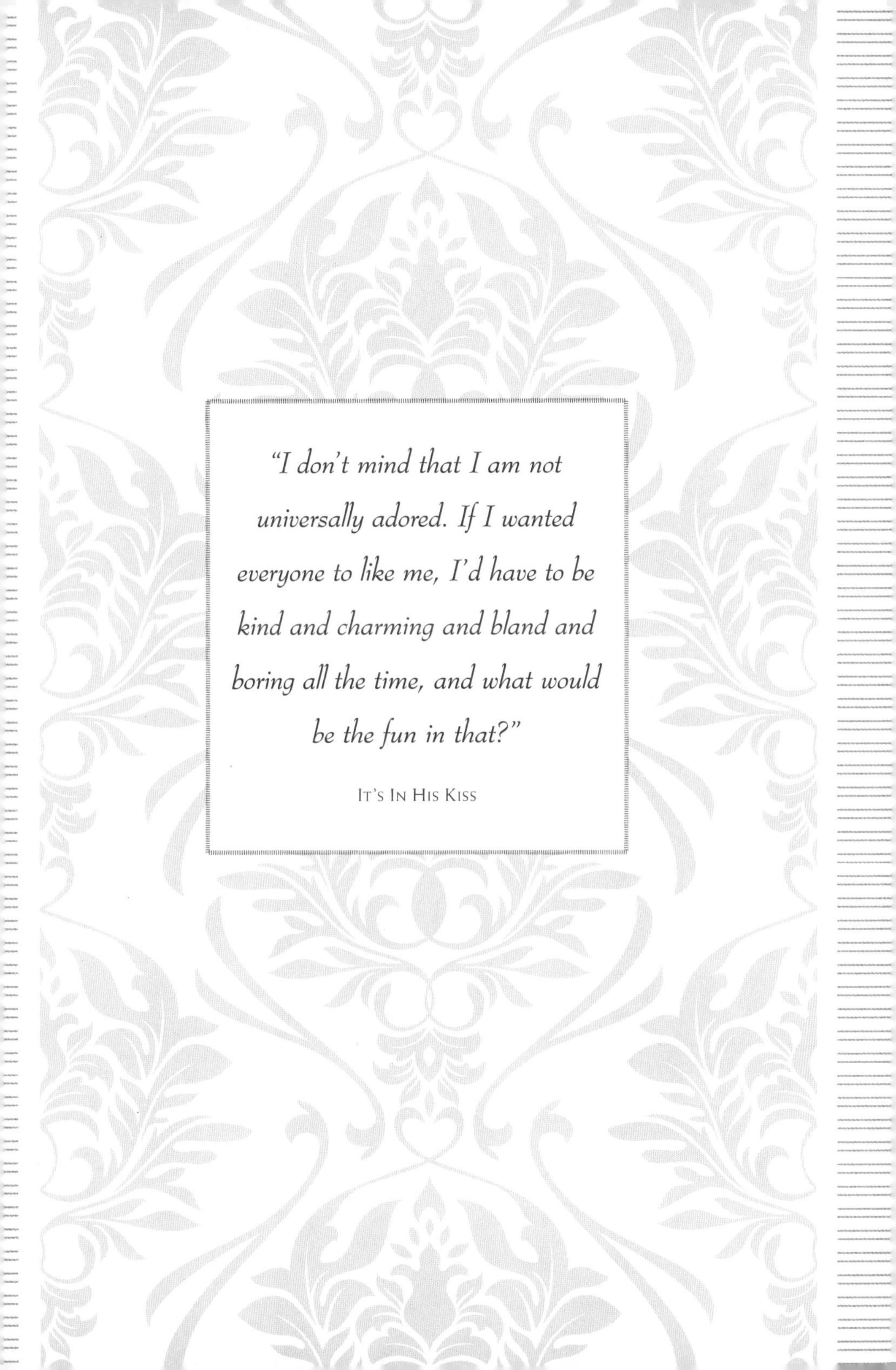

"I don't mind that I am not universally adored. If I wanted everyone to like me, I'd have to be kind and charming and bland and boring all the time, and what would be the fun in that?"

It's In His Kiss

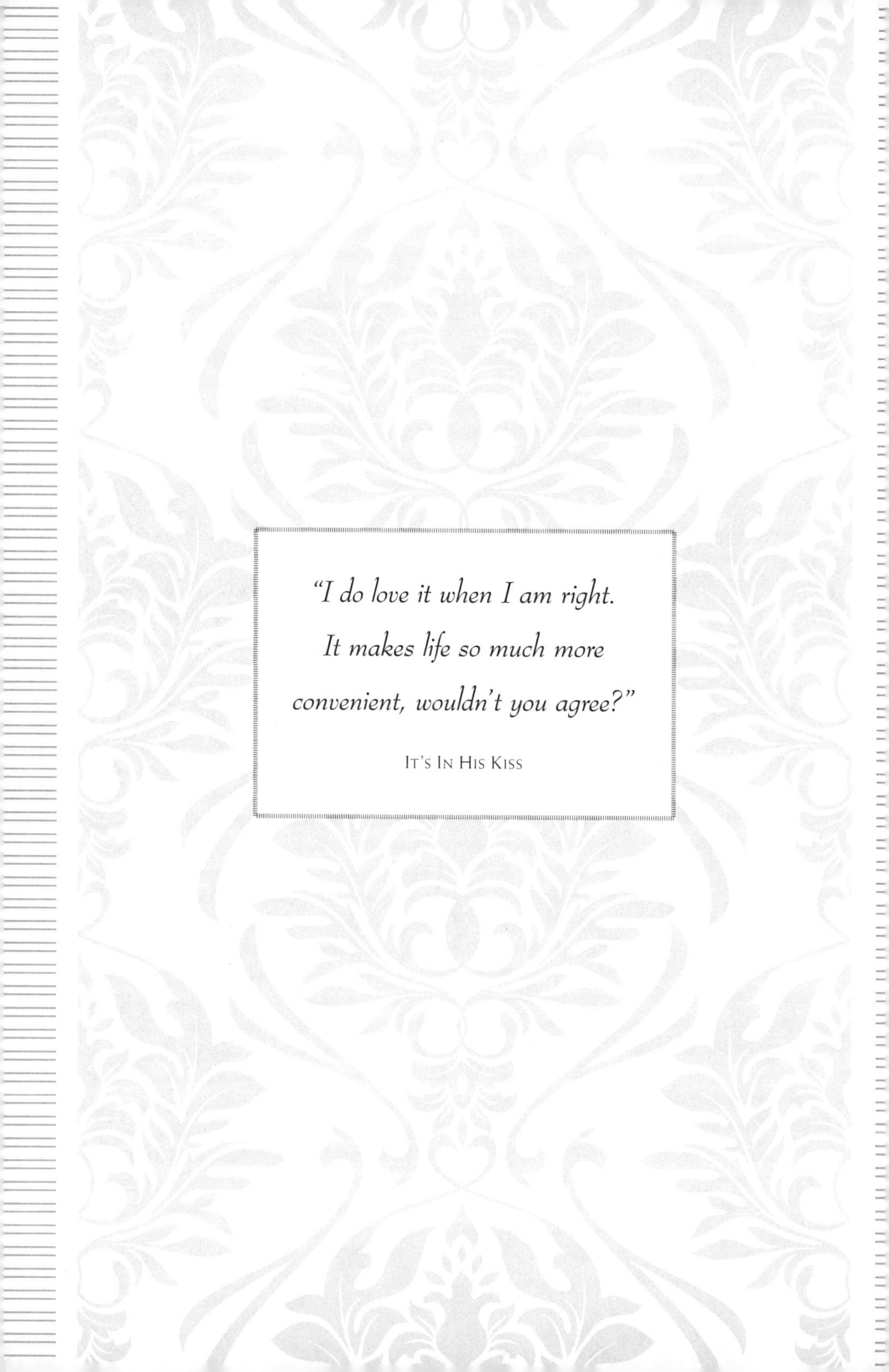

*"I do love it when I am right.
It makes life so much more
convenient, wouldn't you agree?"*

IT'S IN HIS KISS

"What are you talking about?" Hyacinth asked.

"If you don't know," Lady Danbury said loftily, "then you haven't been paying attention, and shame on you for that."

Hyacinth's mouth fell open. "Well," she said, since the alternative was to say nothing, and she never liked to do *that*.

"Why have you not married?" Violet repeated. "Do you even want to?"

"Of course I do." And she did. She wanted it more than she would ever admit, probably more than she'd ever realized until that very moment. She looked at her mother and she saw a matriarch, a woman who loved her family with a fierceness that brought tears to her eyes. And in that moment Hyacinth realized that she wanted to love with that fierceness. She wanted children. She wanted a family.

But that did not mean that she was willing to marry the first man who came along. Hyacinth was nothing if not pragmatic; she'd be happy to marry someone she didn't love, provided he suited her in almost every other respect. But good heavens, was it so much to ask for a gentleman with some modicum of intelligence?

"She's quite diabolical," Gregory said. "It's probably why we can't seem to get her married off."

"Gregory!" This came from Hyacinth, but that was only because Lady Bridgerton had excused herself and had followed one of the footmen into the hall.

"It's a compliment!" Gregory protested. "Haven't you waited your entire life for me to agree that you're smarter than any of the poor fools who have attempted to court you?"

"You might find it difficult to believe," Hyacinth shot back, "but I haven't been going to bed each night thinking to myself—*Oh, I do wish my brother would offer me something that passes for a compliment in his twisted mind.*"

"Why is it," Penelope asked, "that I am left with the feeling that you are keeping score of something, and when I least expect it, you will jump out in front of me, demanding a favor?"

Hyacinth looked at her and blinked. "Why would I need to jump?"

Lady Danbury thumped her cane against the floor, narrowly missing Hyacinth's right foot. "I say," she said, "have either of you caught sight of my grandson?"

"Which grandson?" Hyacinth asked.

"Which grandson," Lady D echoed impatiently. "Which grandson? The only one I like, that's which."

Hyacinth didn't even bother to hide her shock. "Mr. St. Clair is coming tonight?"

"I know, I know," Lady D cackled. "I can hardly believe it myself. I keep waiting for a shaft of heavenly light to burst through the ceiling."

Penelope's nose crinkled. "I think that might be blasphemous, but I'm not sure."

"It's not," Hyacinth said, without even looking at her. "And why is he coming?"

Lady Danbury smiled slowly. Like a snake. "Why are you so interested?"

"I'm *always* interested in gossip," Hyacinth said quite candidly. "About anyone. You should know that already."

"And I know," she said, letting out a short, staccato breath, the sort one did when one couldn't quite believe what one was saying, "that it's often rather hard work to love me."

And suddenly Gareth realized that some things did come in a flash. And there were some things one simply knew without being able to explain them. Because as he stood there watching her, all he could think was—*No.*

No.

It would be rather easy to love Hyacinth Bridgerton.

He didn't know where the thought had come from, or what strange corner of his brain had come to that conclusion, because he was quite certain it would be nearly impossible to *live* with her, but somehow he knew that it wouldn't be at all difficult to love her.

Gareth turned to Gregory. "Your sister will be safe with me," he said. "I give you my vow."

"Oh, I have no worries on that score," Gregory said with a bland smile. "The real question is—will you be safe with her?"

WHEN HE WAS WICKED

"It's not polite to gossip, Hyacinth," Violet said.

"It isn't gossip," Hyacinth retorted. "It's the honest dissemination of information."

HYACINTH, ACCORDING TO HER FAMILY . . .

. . . I grant that Mr. Wilson's face does have a certain amphibious quality, but I do wish you would learn to be a bit more circumspect in your speech. While I would never consider him an acceptable candidate for marriage, he is certainly not a toad, and it ill-behooved me to have my younger sister call him thus, and in his presence.

FROM ELOISE BRIDGERTON TO HER SISTER HYACINTH,
UPON REFUSING HER FOURTH OFFER OF MARRIAGE

To Sir Phillip, With Love

"I don't torture Hyacinth because I *like* to," Gregory said. "I do it because it is *necessary*."

"To whom?"

"To all Britain," he said. "Trust me."

On the Way to the Wedding

"You married into the family," Hyacinth said. "You have to love me. It's a contractual obligation."

"Funny how I don't recall that in the wedding vows."

"Funny," Hyacinth returned, "I remember it perfectly."

Penelope looked at her and then laughed. "I don't know how you do it, Hyacinth," she said, "but exasperating as you are, you somehow always manage to be charming."

It's In His Kiss

"You know I love you dearly, Hyacinth, but you do like to have the upper hand in the conversation."

VIOLET, *It's In His Kiss*

VIOLET

Violet Bridgerton might be the *ton*'s favorite mama. She is legendary in her desire to see her brood happily married, and indeed she has dispatched four of them into the bonds of wedded bliss. But, Dear Reader, those four are merely four of eight, and it does not require a first in mathematics to understand that she is but halfway to her goal.

Will Lady Bridgerton inch closer to the finish line this season? This Author hesitates to predict, but if pressed, would come down on the side of unlikely. Her two youngest—Gregory and Hyacinth—are surely not yet of an age to marry. And the other two who are as yet unwed—Colin and Eloise—display no inclination to do so.

But surely Lady Bridgerton must find comfort and delight in her ever-growing gaggle of grandchildren. Seven at last count: four from the Duke and Duchess of Hastings, two from Viscount and Viscountess Bridgerton, and one from Mr. and Mrs. Benedict Bridgerton. (The names, for those who value such information, are: Amelia, Belinda, Charlotte, David, Edmund, Miles, and Charles.)

Ah, but did I say seven? Just moments before this column was sent to press, This Author caught a whiff of a rumor: Sophie Bridgerton is expecting her second child. Congratulations to Grandmama Violet!

LADY WHISTLEDOWN'S SOCIETY PAPERS, 1819

AN OFFER FROM A GENTLEMAN

"Thank you for dancing with Penelope," Violet said pointedly.

Benedict gave her a rather ironic half-smile. They both knew that her words were meant as a reminder, not as thanks.

THE DUKE AND I

"I don't like your tone" was Violet's standard answer when one of her children was winning an argument.

IT'S IN HIS KISS

"And besides that," Hyacinth added, thinking about the way Mr. St. Clair always seemed to look at her in that vaguely condescending manner of his, "I don't think he likes me very much."

"Nonsense," Violet said, with all the outrage of a mother hen. "Everyone likes you."

Hyacinth thought about that for a moment. "No," she said, "I don't think everyone does."

"Hyacinth, I am your mother, and I know—"

"Mother, you're the *last* person anyone would tell if they didn't like me."

THE DUKE AND I

Violet blinked rapidly, and Daphne noticed that there were actually tears in her mother's eyes. No one ever gave her flowers, she realized. At least not since her father had died ten years earlier. Violet was such a mother—Daphne had forgotten that she was a woman as well.

WHEN HE WAS WICKED

"Oh, it's not your mother's fault," Lady D said. "She's not to blame for the overpopulation of dullards in our society. Good God, she bred eight of you, and not an idiot in the lot." She gave Francesca a pertinent glance. "That's a compliment, by the way."

TO SIR PHILLIP, WITH LOVE

Violet always seemed to know just what her children needed, which was remarkable, really, since there were eight of them—eight very different souls, each with unique hopes and dreams.

The Bridgertons are by far the most prolific family in the upper echelons of society. Such industriousness on the part of the viscountess and the late viscount is commendable, although one can find only banality in their choice of names for their children. Anthony, Benedict, Colin, Daphne, Eloise, Francesca, Gregory, and Hyacinth—orderliness is, of course, beneficial in all things, but one would think that intelligent parents would be able to keep their children straight without needing to alphabetize their names.

LADY WHISTLEDOWN'S SOCIETY PAPERS
26 APRIL 1813

IT'S IN HIS KISS

"Mother," Hyacinth said with a great show of solicitude, "you know I love you dearly—"

"Why is it," Violet pondered, "that I have come to expect nothing good when I hear a sentence beginning in that manner?"

AN OFFER FROM A GENTLEMAN

"It's not my fault all my children ended up looking remarkably alike."

"If the blame can't be placed with you," Benedict asked, "then where may we place it?"

"Entirely upon your father," Lady Bridgerton replied jauntily. She turned to Sophie. "They all look just like my late husband."

IT'S IN HIS KISS

"But that's not what I'm trying to tell you," Violet said, her eyes taking on a slightly determined expression. "What I'm trying to say is that when you were born, and they put you into my arms—it's strange, because for some reason I was so convinced you would look just like your father. I thought for certain I would look down and see his face, and it would be some sort of sign from heaven."

Hyacinth's breath caught as she watched her, and she wondered why her mother had never told her this story. And why she'd never asked.

"But you didn't," Violet continued. "You looked rather like me. And then—oh my, I remember this as if it were yesterday—you looked into my eyes, and you blinked. Twice."

"Twice?" Hyacinth echoed, wondering why this was important.

"Twice." Violet looked at her, her lips curving into a funny little smile. "I only remember it because you looked so deliberate. It was the strangest thing. You gave me a look as if to say, 'I know exactly what I'm doing.' "

A little burst of air rushed past Hyacinth's lips, and she realized it was a laugh. A small one, the kind that takes a body by surprise.

"And then you let out a *wail*," Violet said, shaking her head. "My heavens, I thought you were going to shake the paint right off the walls. And I smiled. It was the first time since your father died that I smiled."

Violet took a breath, then reached for her tea. Hyacinth watched as her mother composed herself, wanting desperately to ask her to continue, but somehow knowing the moment called for silence.

For a full minute Hyacinth waited, and then finally her mother said, softly, "And from that moment on, you were so dear to me. I love all my children, but you . . ." She looked up, her eyes catching Hyacinth's. "You saved me."

"Any man, you'll soon learn, has an insurmountable need to blame someone else when he is made to look a fool."

THE DUKE AND I

❁

"I was so sad. I can't even begin to tell you how sad. There's a kind of grief that just eats you up. It weighs you down. And you can't—" Violet stopped, and her lips moved, the corners tightening in that way they did when a person was swallowing . . . and trying not to cry. "Well, you can't do anything. There's no way to explain it unless you've felt it yourself."

WHEN HE WAS WICKED

"Why did you never remarry?"

Violet's lips parted slightly, and to Francesca's great surprise, her eyes grew bright. "Do you know," Violet said softly, "this is the first time any of you have asked me that?"

"That can't be true," Francesca said. "Are you certain?"

Violet nodded. "None of my children has asked me. I would have remembered."

"No, no, of course you would," Francesca said quickly. But it was all so . . . odd. And unthinking, really. Why would no one have asked Violet about this? It seemed to Francesca quite the most burning question imaginable. And even if none of Violet's children had cared about the answer for their own personal curiosity, didn't they realize how important it was to Violet?

Didn't they want to *know* their mother? Truly know her?

TO SIR PHILLIP, WITH LOVE

Violet Bridgerton had never wanted for anything, but her true wealth lay in her wisdom and her love, and it occurred to Eloise, as she watched Violet turn back to the door, that she was more than just her mother—she was everything that Eloise aspired to be.

And Eloise couldn't believe it had taken her this long to realize it.

ON THE WAY TO THE WEDDING

Violet rolled her eyes. "Every day I marvel that the two of you managed to reach adulthood."

"Afraid we'd kill each other?" Gregory quipped.

"No, that I'd do the job myself."

ROMANCING MISTER BRIDGERTON

"I know, I know," Hyacinth said unrepentantly, "I must be more ladylike."

"If you know it," Violet said, sounding every inch the mother she was, "then why don't you *do* it?"

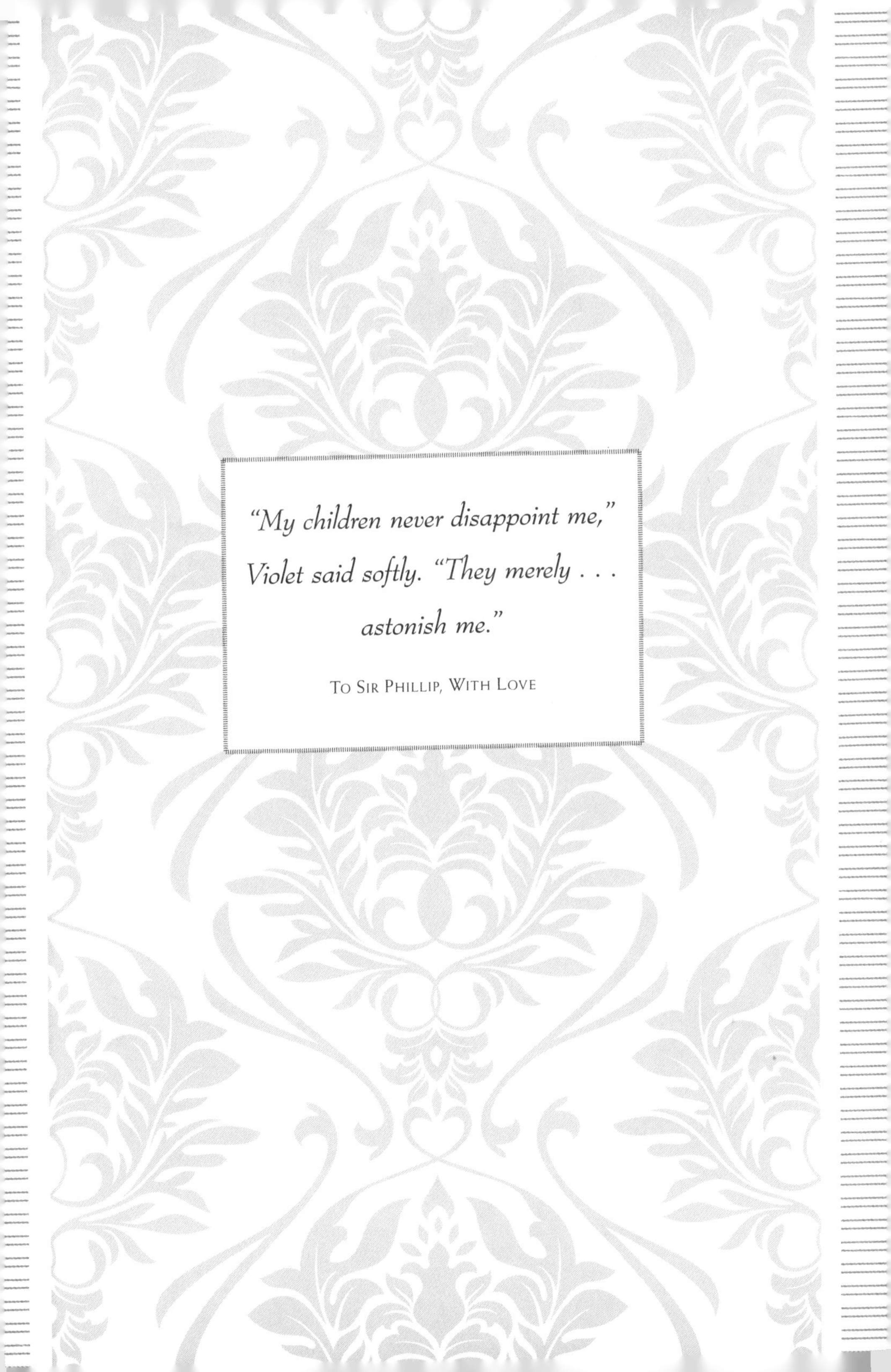
"My children never disappoint me," Violet said softly. "They merely . . . astonish me."
To Sir Phillip, With Love

TO SIR PHILLIP, WITH LOVE

"What did you say to the children?" Phillip immediately asked.

"I don't know," Eloise said quite honestly. "I just tried to act like my mother." She shrugged. "It seemed to work."

THE DUKE AND I

But Hyacinth Bridgerton, who at ten should have known the least about kisses of anyone, just blinked thoughtfully and said, "I think it's nice. If they're laughing now, they'll probably be laughing forever." She turned to her mother. "Isn't that a good thing?"

Violet took her youngest daughter's hand and squeezed it. "Laughter is always a good thing, Hyacinth. And thank you for reminding us of that."

VIOLET, ACCORDING TO HER FAMILY . . .

"It's the curse of motherhood. You're required
to love us even when we vex you."

DAPHNE, *The Duke and I*

Forget Joan of Arc. Her mother was Violet of Mayfair,
and neither plague nor pestilence nor perfidious paramour
would stop her in her quest to see all eight of
her children happily married.

It's In His Kiss

*. . . I do not tell you often enough, dear Mother, how very
grateful I am that I am yours. It is a rare parent who
would offer a child such latitude and understanding.
It is an even rarer one who calls a daughter friend.
I do love you, dear Mama.*

FROM ELOISE BRIDGERTON TO HER MOTHER,
UPON REFUSING HER SIXTH OFFER OF MARRIAGE

To Sir Phillip, With Love

LADY DANBURY

The topic of today's column is, shockingly, Lady Danbury's cat. Surely all have heard of the infamous feline and the dowager countess's blind devotion to the creature that others have described as "appalling," "tyrannical," or even "worth crossing the street to avoid."

(Writing this, it does occur to This Author that these phrases might also be applied to Lady Danbury herself.)

It does seem, however, that the beast was recently unwell. This Author has it on the best authority that Lady Danbury sent her regrets for attendance upon the Hastings Afternoon Tea, letting the former Miss Bridgerton (that would be D for Daphne, now D for Duchess), know that she was needed by her cat.

The Marchioness of Riverdale (that would be E for Elizabeth, possibly now E for embarrassed) visibly winced at the mention of Lady Danbury's feline, whipping her beautifully coiffed blond head from side to side as she uttered a loud and fearful "where?"

Lady Danbury was back to her usual haunts a few days later, however, assuring all who would listen—and indeed, who could have a choice?—that her furry companion (that would be F for feline, probably also F for feared) was back to its usual hale and hearty self.

LADY WHISTLEDOWN'S SOCIETY PAPERS, 1816

IT'S IN HIS KISS

Lesson Number One in dealings with Lady Danbury: Never show weakness.

Lesson Number Two being, of course: When in doubt, refer to Lesson Number One.

THE DUKE AND I

Lady Danbury's brows rose, and when she was but four feet away from the group of Bridgertons, she stopped and barked, "Don't pretend you don't see me!"

IT'S IN HIS KISS

"I have no patience with this current fashion for *ennui*," Lady Danbury continued, reaching for her cane and thumping it against the floor. "Ha. When did it become a crime to show an interest in things?"

THIS AUTHOR would be remiss if it was not mentioned that the most talked-about moment at last night's birthday ball at Bridgerton House was not the rousing toast to Lady Bridgerton (age not to be revealed) but rather Lady Danbury's impertinent offer of one thousand pounds to whomever unmasks . . .

Me.

Do your worst, ladies and gentlemen of the *ton*. You haven't a prayer of solving this mystery.

LADY WHISTLEDOWN'S SOCIETY PAPERS
12 APRIL 1824

THE VISCOUNT WHO LOVED ME

"The world would be a much happier place if people would just listen to me before they up and got married. I could have the entire Marriage Mart matched up in a week."

THE DUKE AND I

"I'd nip that one in the bud, were I you, Miss Bridgerton."

"Did you tell Mr. Berbrooke where I was?"

Lady Danbury's mouth slid into a sly, conspiratorial smile. "I always knew I liked you. And no, I did not tell him where you were."

"Thank you," Daphne said gratefully.

"It'd be a waste of a good mind if you were shackled to that nitwit," Lady Danbury said, "and the good Lord knows that the *ton* can't afford to waste the few good minds we've got."

IT'S IN HIS KISS

Lady Danbury turned back to Hyacinth, her face creasing into what might have been a smile. "I've always liked you, Hyacinth Bridgerton."

"I've always liked you, too," Hyacinth replied.

"I expect it is because you come and read to me from time to time," Lady Danbury said.

"Every week," Hyacinth reminded her.

"Time to time, every week . . . pfft." Lady Danbury's hand cut a dismissive wave through the air. "It's all the same if you're not making it a daily endeavor."

ROMANCING MISTER BRIDGERTON

"Lady Danbury!" Penelope called out, hurrying to the elderly lady's side. "How nice to see you."

"Nobody ever thinks it's nice to see me," Lady Danbury said sharply, "except maybe my nephew, and half the time I'm not even sure about him. But I thank you for lying all the same."

WHEN HE WAS WICKED

"Lady Danbury," Francesca said, "how nice to see you. Are you enjoying yourself this evening?"

Lady D thumped her cane against the ground for no apparent reason. "I'd enjoy myself a dashed sight more if someone would tell me how old your mother is."

"I wouldn't dare."

"Pfft. What's the fuss? It's not as if she's as old as I am."

"And how old are *you*?" Francesca asked, her tone as sweet as her smile was sly.

Lady D's wrinkled face cracked into a smile. "Heh heh heh, clever one you are. Don't think I'm going to tell *you*."

"Then surely you will understand if I exercise the same loyalty toward my mother."

"Hmmph," Lady Danbury grunted, by way of a response, thumping her cane against the floor for emphasis. "What's the use of a birthday party if no one knows what we're celebrating?"

ROMANCING MISTER BRIDGERTON

"Lady Danbury, how nice to see you."

"Heh heh heh." Lady Danbury's wrinkled face became almost young again from the force of her smile. "It's always nice to see me, regardless of what anyone else says."

"My aim in life," Lady Danbury announced, "is to be a menace to as great a number of people as possible."

It's In His Kiss

THE VISCOUNT WHO LOVED ME

"Bridgerton! I say, Bridgerton! Stop at once. I'm speaking to you!"

Anthony groaned as he turned about. Lady Danbury, the dragon of the *ton*. There was simply no way he could ignore her. He had no idea how old she was. Sixty? Seventy? Whatever her age, she was a force of nature, and *no one* ignored her.

"Lady Danbury," he said, trying not to sound resigned as he reined in his mount. "How nice to see you."

ROMANCING MISTER BRIDGERTON

"Miss Featherington!" Lady Danbury said, thumping her cane an inch away from Penelope's foot as soon as she reached her side. "Not you," she said to Felicity, even though Felicity had done nothing more than smile politely as the countess had approached. "You," she said to Penelope.

"Er, good evening, Lady Danbury," Penelope said, which she considered an admirable number of words under the circumstances.

"I have been looking for you all evening," Lady D announced.

Penelope found that a trifle surprising. "You have?"

"Yes. I want to talk with you about that Whistledown woman's last column."

"Me?"

"Yes, you," Lady Danbury grumbled. "I'd be happy to talk with someone else if you could find me a body with more than half a brain."

IT'S IN HIS KISS

"Oh, very well," Lady Danbury said, sounding exceedingly grumpy, which, for her, was exceeding indeed. "I won't say another word."

"Ever?"

"Until," Lady D said firmly.

"Until when?" Hyacinth asked suspiciously.

"I don't know," Lady Danbury replied, in much the same tone.

ROMANCING MISTER BRIDGERTON

"This is the best thing I have ever seen," Eloise said in a gleeful whisper. "Maybe I am a bad person at heart, because I have never before felt such happiness at another person's downfall."

"Balderdash!" Lady Danbury said. "I *know* I am not a bad person, and I find this delightful."

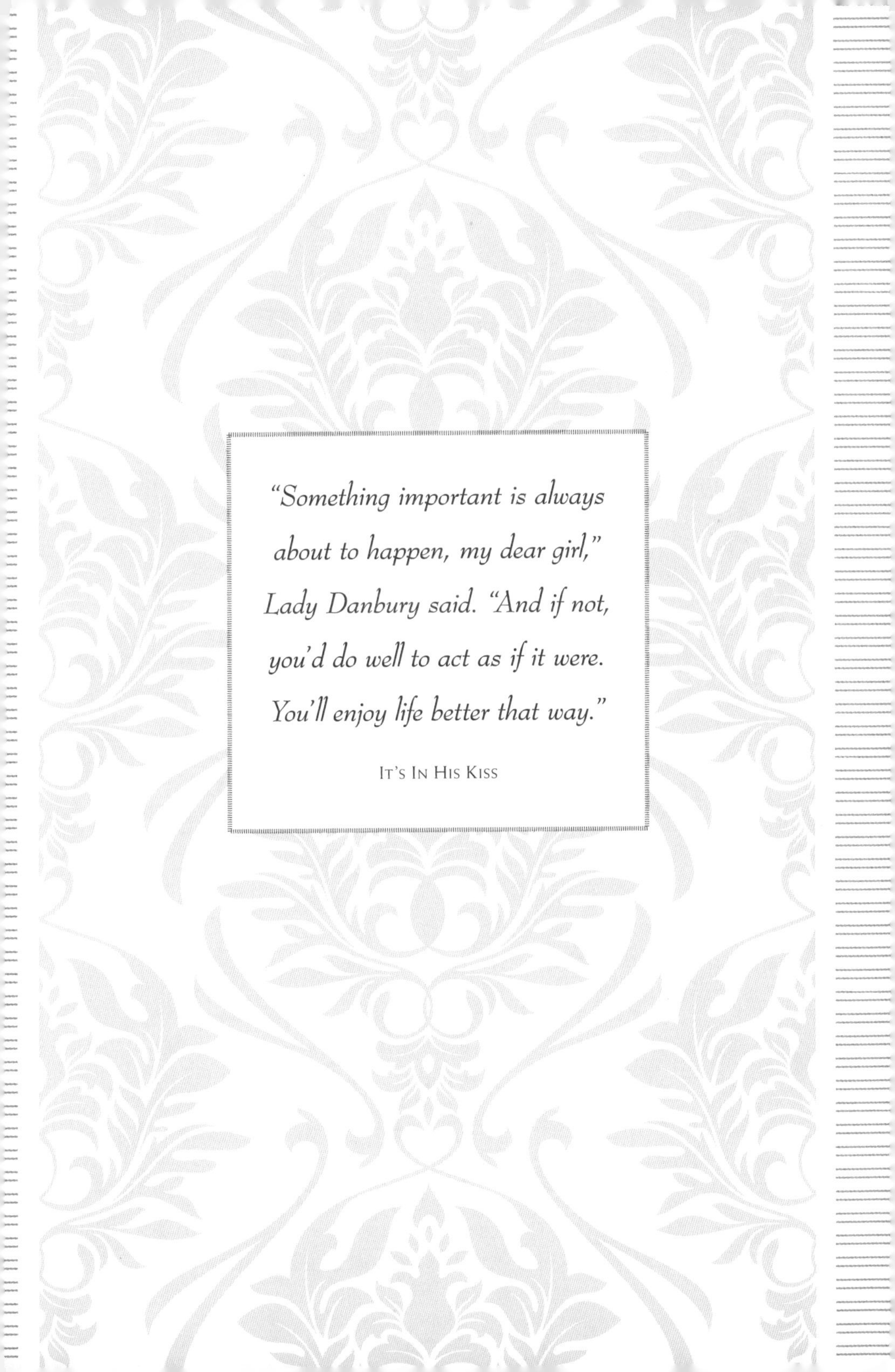

“Something important is always about to happen, my dear girl,” Lady Danbury said. “And if not, you’d do well to act as if it were. You’ll enjoy life better that way.”

It’s In His Kiss

"You sound like Lady Danbury," Violet said.

"I like Lady Danbury," Hyacinth replied.

"I like her, too, but that doesn't mean I want her as my daughter."

"Isn't patience a virtue?"

"Absolutely not," Lady Danbury said emphatically, "and if you think so, you're less of a woman than I thought."

"When I die," Gareth said, "surely my epitaph will read, 'He loved his grandmother when no one else would.' "

"And what's wrong with that?" Lady Danbury asked.

"Hyacinth," he said.

She looked at him expectantly.

"Hyacinth," he said again, this time with a bit more certitude. He smiled, letting his eyes melt into hers. "Hyacinth."

"We *know* her name," came his grandmother's voice.

Gareth ignored her and pushed a table aside so that he could drop to one knee. "Hyacinth," he said, relishing her gasp as he took her hand in his, "would you do me the very great honor of becoming my wife?"

Her eyes widened, then misted, and her lips, which he'd been kissing so deliciously mere hours earlier, began to quiver. "I . . . I . . ."

It was unlike her to be so without words, and he was enjoying it, especially the show of emotion on her face.

"I . . . I . . ."

"Yes!" his grandmother finally yelled. "Yes! She'll marry you!"

"She can speak for herself," he said.

"No," Lady D said, "she can't. Quite obviously."

"You're going to be my grandmother," Hyacinth said, leaning down and giving her a kiss on the cheek. She'd never assumed such familiarity before, but somehow it felt right.

"You silly child," Lady Danbury said, brushing at her eyes as Hyacinth walked to the door. "In my heart, I've been your grandmother for years. I've just been waiting for you to make it official."

THE BRIDGERTON SERIES

The Duke and I

The Viscount Who Loved Me

An Offer From a Gentleman

Romancing Mister Bridgerton

To Sir Phillip, With Love

When He Was Wicked

It's In His Kiss

On the Way to the Wedding

The Bridgertons: Happily Ever After